Your Nostalgia Is Killing Me

Your Nostalgia Is Killing Me

Linked Stories

* * *

JOHN WEIR

Red Hen Press | *Pasadena, CA*

This book is the Winner of the 2020 Grace Paley Prize in Short Fiction. AWP is a national nonprofit organization dedicated to serving American letters, writers, and programs of writing. AWP's headquarters are at Riverdale Park, Maryland.

Book design by Mark E. Cull

Library of Congress Cataloging-in-Publication Data

Names: Weir, John, 1959– author.
Title: Your nostalgia is killing me : linked stories / John Weir.
Description: First edition. | Pasadena, CA : Red Hen Press, [2022]
Identifiers: LCCN 2021023695 (print) | LCCN 2021023696 (ebook) | ISBN 9781636280295 (trade paperback) | ISBN 9781636280301 (epub)
Subjects: LCGFT: Linked stories.
Classification: LCC PS3573.E39745 Y68 2022 (print) | LCC PS3573.E39745 (ebook) | DDC 813/.54—dc23
LC record available at https://lccn.loc.gov/2021023695
LC ebook record available at https://lccn.loc.gov/2021023696

The National Endowment for the Arts, the Los Angeles County Arts Commission, the Ahmanson Foundation, the Dwight Stuart Youth Fund, the Max Factor Family Foundation, the Pasadena Tournament of Roses Foundation, the Pasadena Arts & Culture Commission and the City of Pasadena Cultural Affairs Division, the City of Los Angeles Department of Cultural Affairs, the Audrey & Sydney Irmas Charitable Foundation, the Meta & George Rosenberg Foundation, the Albert and Elaine Borchard Foundation, the Adams Family Foundation, Amazon Literary Partnership, the Sam Francis Foundation, and the Mara W. Breech Foundation partially support Red Hen Press.

First Edition
Published by Red Hen Press
www.redhen.org

Acknowledgments

Ten of these stories were first published elsewhere, often in different versions and with other titles. "American Graffiti" first appeared in *Gulf Coast* as "Tangled Up in Blue." "Scenes from a Marriage" first appeared in *New South*. "Kid A" first appeared in *Bloom*. "Political Funerals" first appeared online in *Lambda Literary*. "The Origin of the Milky Way" first appeared online in *World Literature Today*. "It Must Be Swell to Be Laying Out Dead," as "Dave Shaking," first appeared in the collection *Vital Signs: Essential AIDS Fiction*. "Katherine Mansfield" first appeared in *Subtropics*, as did "Humoresque," as "Hurts." "Neorealism at the Infiniplex" and "It Gets Worse" include passages from my novel *What I Did Wrong*.

Thanks to the editors at the above publications: Richard Canning, Laurie Ann Cedilnik, Charles Flowers, Wesley Gibson, George Henson, Michelle Johnson, William Johnson, Mike Jones, Rick Kot, David Leavitt, James Davis May, Giuseppe Taurino, and Sasha West.

Thanks also and especially to the Association of Writers and Writing Programs (AWP) for sponsoring the Grace Paley Prize for Short Fiction, and to Amina Gautier for naming this collection its 2020 recipient; and to Mark E. Cull, Kate Gale, Natasha McClellan, Tobi Harper, and Rebeccah Sanhueza at Red Hen Press. And shoutouts to Ryan Black, Sameer Pandya, Kim Smith, Miles Grier, Lisa Guido, and Wayne Moreland.

For 5,000 Facebook friends and 3,011 followers, at last count
And for Helen Eisenbach, of course

Contents

In this our life there are no beginnings but only departures entitled beginnings, wreathed in the formal emotions thought to be appropriate and often forced. Darkly rises each moment from the life which has been lived and which does not die, for each event lies in the heavy head forever, waiting to renew itself.

—Delmore Schwartz
from his novella, *The World Is a Wedding*

AIDS Nostalgia

I remember what suits me.

—Robert Ryan in Anthony Mann's *The Naked Spur*,
screenplay by Sam Rolfe and Harold Jack Bloom

Neorealism at the Infiniplex

My friend Dave died of AIDS in the fall of 1994. I had planned to be sad about it, but it turned out I was relieved. I'm not proud of this. In my fantasy, he would have died in my arms, and the screen would have faded to black, like in a movie. It was an Italian neorealist ending, a grim death but a noble one, suffered in a time of war or shortly after war. What happened instead was that he was so mean for the last three months of his life that I stopped liking him. Not just at the time, but for all time, both in the season of his death and retroactively, forever. His dying wasted our five years of friendship, and I lost him in retrospect. I don't remember what I ever liked about him. People say they can't believe their beloved husband, mother, son is gone, but I had another feeling. I couldn't convince myself that I had ever known and loved someone named David. That was the worst thing that happened.

No, the worst thing was that he left me some money that took a long time to clear. In 1997, three years after he died, I got about three thousand dollars, and I decided to rent a place in upstate New York. Because I teach school, I have my summers free, and I sublet my East Village apartment, bought a used car at a police auction in Jamaica, Queens, and signed a three-month lease on a converted chicken coop. It was on the grounds of an old Dutch farm, and it was vast and cheap, with a high ceiling and a sleeping loft. There was no furniture, so I bought a futon mattress and a table. I put the table in the kitchen in front of a window with a view of the mountains. On the table, I set a laptop and a stack of books I had never finished reading: *Paradise Lost*,

Proust, *War and Peace*. I was going to read the classics, write things, eat right, go running every afternoon on the back roads and country lanes, and finally lose the weight I'd gained while Dave was dying.

Of course, I hate back roads and country lanes. How had I forgotten that? I hate views. I especially dislike chicken coops. Mine still smelled faintly of chickens. When I looked up from my work, through my kitchen window, I could see an open field, trees in the distance, and the sky everywhere. Not the reassuringly manmade chemical sky of lower Manhattan, but an intimidating sky so awesome and inhuman that in order to explain it, you were forced to invent God.

When I fell asleep over *Paradise Lost*, sitting outside in an Adirondack chair that had bark clinging to its arms and legs, I woke scraped and sunburned and covered with bug bites. A mile down the road at the food co-op, the cashier was so vegetarian she would not sell me bug spray. Within days, I was aching for anything lethal or synthetic. I was nostalgic for pizza and car fumes and Avenue A. Of course, there were people living in my apartment—German students on summer holiday—and I couldn't go home.

Twice, I drove down to the city and paid eighty dollars to sleep in the Jungle Room at the Kew Motor Inn. Obviously, I couldn't spend the summer traveling back and forth every day between a New Paltz chicken coop and a by-the-hour motel off the Grand Central Parkway in Queens.

So I loaded Proust and Milton and Tolstoy into the trunk of my car, and I went to the movies.

I moved to the multiplex. To many different multiplexes, which are so abundant in the wilderness that I began to think of all upstate New York as a vast infiniplex. From late June to early September, I went to every several-screen movie theater from Kingston to Yonkers, listening to Billy Joel songs on the car radio and crying because I was old enough to remember liking them without irony. When I was not in my car, I was seated front row center with a bucket of popcorn and a Coke, watching Bruce Willis in *Armageddon*. You see how entertainment was not the point.

If I kept going back to *Armageddon*, I thought, it would eventually turn out to have a plot. I saw it six times, and it never did. I was grateful; it was a relief to be spared the pain of cause/effect. Thank God for a plotless world. Watching the scene where Bruce Willis, draped in an American flag, says goodbye to earth from the floor of a crater in a huge piece of orbiting igneous rock was the most satisfying emotional experience I have ever had. I'm through with stuff that really happens, like people die and you don't. Or they die and you don't feel bad in the way that you want.

Which is how I got in trouble with *Saving Private Ryan*, Steven Spielberg's feel-good D-Day massacre movie. I saw it twelve times. I saw it twice a week for nearly two months, like short-term therapy or a lover who beats you every time you go back, despite your absurd faith that one of these days it will end differently.

Saving Private Ryan is more believable than *Armageddon*—though this, for me, was not the point. I didn't care about World War II. Isn't it a film about a bunch of gay guys in 1983 who take a summer house on Fire Island?

Look at the evidence: it opens with a few hundred handsome young men in expensive outerwear squeezed into a boat approaching the shore of a famous beach, where people casually speak French and stern Nordics are lurking in the dunes with their hands on their weapons. We meet eight guys, just enough for a half-share in the Pines. Most of them are Midwestern. Once ashore, they go from house to house in uniforms, carrying accessories, singing Duke Ellington songs about solitude and haunting and listening to Edith Piaf, all the while searching for just one cute boy. And every few days, one of them dies.

It's the same plot as *Longtime Companion*, one of the first films about AIDS. A bunch of men with no special talent or need for intimacy or closeness have to deal with the fact that everyone they know is dying all around them all the time. Sometimes they abandon their dead. Sometimes they mourn them. They do what they can, given their uneasy sense that the next person dead could be you. Later, the dead men are buried far from their hometowns, out of sight of their folks, gone in a way their parents can't, or won't, understand.

When Dave died, his mom and dad came up from Florida in a rental car. He died on Wednesday and was buried on Friday. They left their house Thursday morning and drove, they said, straight through. Nonetheless, they were two hours late for the funeral service at Riverside Memorial Chapel on the Upper West Side of Manhattan. The service had to be finished by sundown because he was Jewish, it was Friday afternoon, and the parents had insisted long-distance—even though David hated God or even the mention of God—that there be religious last rites.

So we waited in the chapel. It was the fifth time I had been there for a dead friend. We went through two rabbis. Each of them stayed an hour and then had to leave. The place was rented; it was full. David was naked in a pine box loaded with ice to keep the body from stinking. The coffin was sweating as the ice was slowly dissolving. We had a bucket under the corner to catch the drips. I thought of Dave floating inside this cocktail like a lemon wedge. All the mourners, David's friends and coworkers and cute guys from the Chelsea gym, were sitting quietly in the pews listening to the drip, drop, drip into the bucket.

The stage was set, and the effects were starting to melt, and we had no parents, and now suddenly, no rabbi.

Try finding a rabbi free on Friday afternoon on the Upper West Side of Manhattan. I made an announcement in the chapel, really a plea. "Does anybody here know . . . ?" How would I ask it? I felt in need of Mel Brooks. He would have struck the right tone. But it turned out that somebody had a cousin who knew somebody, who knew somebody . . . And I made the calls. "We've never met, but I need a rabbi."

It took ten calls. The sun was setting. Thank God some Jews are not observant; people were answering their phones. Finally, we got a rabbi. I never said, "AIDS." I didn't know what to say about AIDS. I wasn't sure he'd do it. I said nothing. I said, "Dead guy on ice," which sounds like a hard-core band. And he understood; he came to the chapel. Why wasn't he busy on a Friday night? I didn't want to know. Cut-rate rabbi. Though he cost just as much as the other two. Charged for three, used one. Not the star, but the understudy. We paid for Nathan Lane, we got Steve Guttenberg instead—fine. He's available.

He showed up five minutes ahead of Dave's parents. Their rental car had broken down in Philadelphia. Never mind that the quickest route is not through Philadelphia. That's why God gave us the New Jersey Turnpike. Turn right at Wilmington, you're in Jersey. Why tour Philadelphia? Whatever. I had avoidances of my own. Just before the parents appeared, the rabbi took me into a small room and said, "Quick, tell me about your friend. Say what he was like. Say three things. I don't need more than three. Add some color, make it personal, and make it fast."

And all I could think to say was, "Well, he spent a lot of time at the gym."

It was the wrong thing to say, that he was just a gym-going muscle queen, a gay cliché. Though it was true, he went to the gym the way Baptists go down to the river. Still, there were plenty of other things to say about him, and why was this my first thought? He was a writer, he had published three books; what kept me from listing these accomplishments? Grief is sneaky, not sobering; it refuses to suppress your worst impulse.

Then the parents appear.

So there is the sudden attention to the parents. Who presumably have precedence. Even though they had not visited David even once, had not in fact seen him in more than a year, hadn't called except when the rates were low on Sundays, and had sent, as a token of their concern, only a single package of home-baked chocolate chip cookies. For a guy who could not digest so much as a piece of dry toast without soiling his shorts. David made me eat the cookies in his hospital room while he swore at his nurses. Then he swore at me. Then he died, and we had a ten-minute funeral service where the parents got front row seats.

The rabbi ripped cloth from their garb in honor of some tradition that did not include my dead friend, who had wanted to have his whole arm tattooed at the last minute so no respectable Jewish cemetery would take him.

Kaddish was said, and the rabbi made some remarks. He said, "David was a man who loved sports, especially at the gym." And a roomful of people, not his parents, burst out laughing because he was famous, at the gym, for cornering cute boys naked in the steam room and asking them to lunch.

The Kaddish was endless. I don't know when I've hated God so much. I had tracked down the last photograph of David taken before he went into the hospital, and we got it blown up, and it was standing on an easel next to the rabbi. An awful picture. Dave looked shrunken and rabbity and pale. He had shaved off his seventies-era Christopher Street gay clone mustache, and though I always hated that mustache, he was unrecognizable without it. He lost more than half his body weight in the two months before he died, and this photograph was how I would always remember him now: a huddle of bones under sacked skin, which happened to be my dying, now dead, friend.

His body had nothing to do with him. His funeral service had nothing to do with anyone who cared for him. It was an appalling farce. I had to be polite to his parents, who, if they loved him at all, could nonetheless not manage to visit their dying son. They knew he was dying. If he were my son, I would have moved into his hospital room. I would have postponed my life to be with him, which is basically what I did. And they were his parents, they sent cookies, I despised them, I wished they had died instead, I hope they die soon, lost and alone and uncared for by their own flesh and blood.

Afterward, we talked like I thought they were human. They barely registered my humanity or my closeness to Dave. They had me down as "good friend," official funeral parlor role. I was not family. It was their loss, not mine, and I had exactly a minute to cry. It happened in a closet. No kidding. I was not going to cry in front of someone's suddenly visible parents. I found a coat closet, oddly empty for November. I thought, Well, as well here as anywhere else. I thought, This is where it turns out I was always going to have my private sorrowing moment. I don't believe in God, but I do believe in the fated emptiness of coat closets and private moments of sequestered grief. I leaned in a corner, folding myself into the crease of a papered wall as if the angle of the building could hold me.

In a minute, I was going to have to walk out into the reception room and answer questions, give directions, to the cemetery in Queens, to the ice-skating rink at Rockefeller Center. That's what the parents wanted to know. They had driven all the way from Florida and they were not leaving without seeing the sights, buying souvenirs, "My Son Died of AIDS and All I Got Was This Lousy T-Shirt." But for now, avoiding them, crouched under coat hooks, I cried; it was almost the only time I cried about AIDS. Half the people I knew when I was twenty-five years old are dead, and I have cried while Dave's parents waited, and I cried at twelve different showings of the last scene of *Saving Private Ryan.*

The scene that Amy Taubin of *The Village Voice* called "creepy."

I thought it was the whole point.

Actually, the popcorn was the point. It was my steady diet. Every chain movie theater sells a Supercombo Special—a huge bag of popcorn and a giant soda—served by an underpaid teen who stares to the left of your head and asks, as slowly as possible, "Do you want the

Special it's only fifty cents more than the medium size the soda comes with free refills—"

And I say, "Yes. Now. Immediately. Please. I want, I want, I want," I say, interrupting, slapping money on the counter, exact change. God forbid I should have to wait for them to make change. Give me a giant size popcorn, I say, soak it in butter to ruin my heart and salt for my tears, so I can taste it on my face hours later when Steven Spielberg makes me watch an old guy walk through acres of white crosses—a military graveyard in France—and drop to his knees in front of the headstone of a friend who died in battle instead of him.

It's the end of *Saving Private Ryan*. World War II's over; we won. Spielberg has returned us to the framing device, a scene taking place more than fifty years after the war, in the present moment, a summer day in 1997. Private Ryan, who was saved by his buddies, is now an old man, no longer played by Matt Damon. He is white-haired, slow-moving, unglamorous. Since the beginning of the film, and presumably all through the two-hour-long flashback to the Second World War, he has been walking with his family, his wife and son, and his son's wife and his grandchildren, up and down the rows of headstones in the military graveyard.

Suddenly, he stops in front of one of the bone-white crosses. The John Williams music swells and an American flag whips overhead—though we're in France. You're right, Amy Taubin, it's schmaltz. I'm moved by schlock. In front of the headstone, the old guy seems to be tossed to his knees by an electrical shock. He is on the ground before the grave, weeping, not dead. He turns to his wife.

"Tell me I'm a good man," he asks her.

His family stands behind him, kind of appalled. They've got no idea what he means. Clearly, he has never mentioned the war or how he was spared, or why his friends died.

His family doesn't have a clue what he's talking about, but I do. He wants them to know what it's like to have the worst thing happen, to lose everything and never discuss it, so that you lose it twice, both in the moment, when it actually goes, and afterward, in the official record of its going. So two things are gone, Dave is gone and you're gone. And maybe you get a moment to cry for what, now, you will never be able to tell: that all the people you loved for a season had died, and that you, for years and years after, quite simply, had not.

American Graffiti

Jodie Foster came out at the Golden Globes by saying she wouldn't.

It was the opposite of a speech act that performs what it says. Her statement performed what it didn't say. What it refused to say. It was like how you'd come out if you were Magritte.

There she is framed in the TV set or computer screen, enacting disclosure, above a caption that reads, This Is Not a Disclosure.

A surrealist says, "I'm gay," but it's in French and it's a collage and the words are scattered across the page in the shape of a teapot.

It was 2013. She was fifty-one years old. "If you had been a public figure from the time that you were a toddler," she said, "maybe you too might value privacy above all else."

And what I want to know is: what's "privacy?"

*** *** ***

It's the bicentennial spring of 1976, America's two-hundredth birthday, and I'm seventeen years old and sitting in a football field, waiting for my name to be called.

I'm at my high school graduation.

My best friend Lottie picked me up this morning and drove me here. She finished school two years ahead of me, but she's around. We split a joint in her car, and she gave me two hits of speed.

"Are you high as a motherfucker?" she said, which was what she liked to say, and I said, "Yes. I believe I am."

Not as high as I want to be, though, because I'm still here. I'm on the planet, in New Jersey, surrounded by kids and cornfields and sitting in the back row of a set of bleachers that somebody—maintenance guys, President Ford, Jesus Son of God—dragged to the fifty-yard line, so five hundred white kids would have somewhere to sit while everyone waited to see what happened when our names were called.

I already know what will happen.

We rehearsed this:

After speeches, after the awarding of prizes from local clubs and business sponsors—Kiwanis Club Prize, Lion's Club Prize, Betty Crocker Homemaker's Prize—after the naming of National Honor Society members, and the best kid's valedictorian address, and the class president's reading of the Class Prophecy, and the class treasurer's reading of the Final Disbursement of Funds, after the national anthem and the school song, after an appearance by the local State Assembly member, and a blessing by both a Presbyterian minister and a Catholic priest—all that, though not in that order—the superintendent will call our names, and we will leave the bleachers, one by one, cross in front of the moms and dads watching from their stadium seats, climb a set of steps to the superintendent, grab his palm and our diploma, turn back down the steps, pass again in front of family and friends, walk behind the bleachers, and circle back to our seats.

It's a beautiful June day. The school building, red brick with white trim, familiar American rural public high school from the 1950s—it opened in the fall of '51—is behind us, spread across a hill, the original structure flanked by jutting additions that show how the north of the county has grown over twenty-five years.

Downhill across the highway is a cornfield that ends in a distant red barn. The highway, Route 31, goes north to Clinton, where two mills, a red mill and a stone mill, face each other across the South Branch of the Raritan River. And it goes south to Flemington, past our rival high school, the Devils. Their colors are red and black. We're the Lions. Our colors are green and gold. Our mortarboards are hung with green tassels that are decorated with little gold Liberty Bells for the bicentennial. When everyone's name has been called, and we have gotten our rolled-up diplomas, we are going to flip our tassels from one side of our mortarboards to the other, at a signal, in unison.

The football field is anchored at either end by green scoreboards that advertise our football team. You can see the white letters, STATE CHAMPS, from the highway.

It's a big high school in a county of farmlands that are turning into subdivisions, the spent farm economy and new consumer economy growing and vanishing inside of each other, in the northern part of the county, at the base of a range of low hills.

The awards have been distributed; the speakers have spoken. The superintendent starts calling names. It takes a while. Nearly five-hundred kids. Sooner than I want, it's my turn. My name is called like everyone else's in a series of echoes from the football field's PA system.

This is what was going to happen, and it does: along with the echoes of my name, you can hear a bunch of kids, freshmen and sophomores mostly, yelling, "Faggot!"

They're in the audience, near my parents. I go down the bleachers to the field, and they yell louder. I walk past the audience, and they keep yelling.

"Faggot!"

"Fairy!"

"Fruitcake!"

"Homo!"

"Girly faggot!"

"Queer!"

Nobody had to rehearse this. It happens all the time. I'm the high school homo. The boy who acts like a girl. I'm called a faggot every day. It starts in the morning when the school bus comes down Route 513, and the kids from Califon are already leaning out the windows two hundred yards away and screaming, "Faggot!" At school, I'm pushed against lockers and punched in hallways and called a faggot on my way from one class to the next. When I get off the school bus at night, kids lean out the windows and scream, "Faggot!" as the bus disappears out of sight.

I have known all along that I would not get past the audience at graduation without being called a faggot, in a chorus of voices, loud enough for everyone to hear.

I walk through the sound of their voices. I go to the superintendent, who shakes my hand and says, "Congratulations," in a low voice that I can nonetheless hear over the sound of—ten, twelve, twenty?—students calling me a faggot. It sounds like a hundred. My parents can hear it. My brother. My brother's girlfriend.

Lottie too?

Is she here?

I can't remember if she said she was going to stay. I could scan the crowd, but I have taught myself never to look up or out when people are calling me queer.

I get my diploma. Then I turn around, back down the steps, past the audience, through the voices, around behind the bleachers, and up to my seat, where I wait for the signal to move my tassel with the Liberty Bell from one side of my head to the other.

* * *

I was a faggot, but I wasn't sure I was gay. I didn't want to be gay because it meant I was a faggot. Yet I would still be a faggot, because I acted like a girl.

Gender categories in rural New Jersey in 1976: boy, girl, faggot.

If I was gay, I was a faggot. If I was not gay, but a girl, I was a faggot. Was I a gay faggot, a faggot and gay? Or was I just a faggot?

Everyone knew I was a faggot, but not everyone thought I was gay.

Most people thought I was gay.

Most people did not include me. Not yet.

And maybe Lottie.

We never talked about it. She didn't ask, I didn't tell.

✳ ✳ ✳

Lottie was my best friend since I was fourteen. She was my rock star and bodyguard, tough, brotherly, and aloof. Her mother was German-from-Germany, and her father was huge and German-Irish and chief of police of Clinton, New Jersey. His name was Chief Gus. Lottie was their only daughter, out of six kids. She had a long straight nose and John Lennon wire-frame granny glasses, and she smoked Camel straights and dressed in blue jeans and T-shirts like a boy. And she had a car. Under cover of her friendship, I could go places where I would not be called a fag.

Even squeezed between two of her five brothers at her mom's dinner table, I felt safe. Not because her dad was a cop. He came to dinner with Caesar, a blue-black German Shepherd with matted fur and hip dysplasia. We ate in silence while Chief Gus shared his food with the dog, and Lottie's mom doled out seconds before our plates were clean.

Her mom must have thought Lottie and I were dating, even though I was a faggot, because the night before my high school graduation, she made a big meal in my honor. Meatloaf, creamed corn, coleslaw, scalloped potatoes, hot rolls, and lemonade. For dessert, she baked a cake. It was more a lesson than a dessert—a bitter chocolate *Schwarzwald* cake with marzipan icing that held it tight. On top was my name in gothic script.

I felt warned. Lottie's mom was Bavarian, and her kitchen was hung with samplers that said *Verboten*. She knew I wanted to get out of New Jersey without saying goodbye. Two days after my graduation, I was leaving for a summer job, and then I was going to college in Ohio.

For the past year, I had been trying not to make an impression, so I could vanish without a trace. Yet Lottie's mom served a cake as dense and heavy as a doorstop.

Despite what her mom suspected or wished, Lottie and I weren't "going steady"; we were potheads. We had gotten high before dinner, and my pupils were spinning plates on a juggler's stick. "Can you please be cool?" Lottie whispered. I could never be cool. Before dessert was done, she grabbed my arm and hurried me out to her hippie car, a blue Volkswagen Beetle, where she lit a joint and headed for the interstate. She never worried about cops because of her dad. Or maybe she was just lucky.

"She baked that thing all day," she was saying, "your cake. Do you know what I got at my high school graduation? I'm the oldest, the first. My mom never graduated high school. You know what I got? From her?" She passed me the joint. "I got to do the dishes, that's what I got." Then she stepped on the gas.

We were going to Oldwick. Our friend Cindy was throwing a party while her parents were gone, and she wanted us to meet her new boyfriend Greg, an older kid, college boy from Princeton, who had pot to sell: Colombian weed, my graduation present.

We were celebrating, but not yet. Lottie was pissed off. "My father's goddamned dog," she was saying. "He's such an asshole." Her *esses* hissed like Satan's. I loved her abrading voice, which I felt up the back of my neck. She hardly wasted her scorn on anything she didn't love. "He eats cake off his plate and it gives him the runs," she said. It wasn't clear whether she meant Dad or the dog: who fed whom, who got the runs, which one of them was the asshole? "He thinks he's Jesus."

"Who? Caesar? Your dad's dog is Jesus?"

"No, not the dog," she said, punching me in the arm. Days later, I noticed a small bruise. "You're all so hangdog," she said, "like him."

We never fought. Were we fighting now? I wasn't sure. What if we were? I started to sing "On the Street Where You Live." It was from

My Fair Lady, the spring musical at our high school the year we met. Lottie was the stage manager. I was on the stage crew. The guy who sang "On the Street Where You Live" looked like Bobby Sherman in *Here Come the Brides*.

"Oh my fucking God," Lottie said. "He never got that song right."

"People clapped."

"People clap at dog acts."

"What kind? Like eating Mom's *Schwarzwald* cake off the plate?"

That did it. We fell into a laughing jag. The trigger was "*Schwarzwald*." We laughed so hard she swerved off the road, but I wasn't scared. She got back on track fast. I had ridden with Lottie when we were high on everything from hash to tequila, and we always got home.

"Jesus—" she said.

"—is somebody's dog," I said, finishing her sentence, not blinking as she swerved, proving I could be cool.

"Don't blaspheme in my car," she said, crossing herself, which she both meant and didn't. "I never called anyone Jesus. I said, 'He thinks he's Jesus.'"

"So does Jesus."

"Will you shut up?"

"That's the trouble with Jesus," I said, repeating something I heard my mother say. "What if Jesus was just one of those guys who thinks he's Jesus?"

That silenced us. We didn't speak again until we got off the highway. Lottie took the exit ramp, and we were on the Oldwick Road. We lowered our windows and felt the damp air, full of the scent of pine sap and red clay dirt, and the ammoniac smell of dung rising from the low hills that rolled into corn rows and pasture for cattle. "Everything is ripe here," I said accusingly. Then Lottie pulled to a Stop sign and turned to me.

"Where do we go now?" she said. She sounded angry, not lost.

For the first time, I wondered if she was upset about my leaving.

I had never asked. I went blank around Lottie, especially when we got high. She let me disappear. What if she had been waiting all this time for me to, you know, "start something?" Wow, that seemed unlikely. I looked out the window. We were in front of the Oldwick Public Library, where we had once sat on folding metal chairs before a collapsible screen and watched a bad print of *Bonnie and Clyde*. Faye Dunaway and Warren Beatty as platonic lovers. Was that Lottie and me? The whole point of our friendship was not to think about sex. We had an unspoken agreement that she protected me from mean guys, and I would never grab her breasts. She said breasts were a dartboard under your chin.

Was I supposed to "make a move"? Even the words were ridiculous. It was how her brothers talked. Maybe it's what her mom's cake meant. Lottie's rage at her dad's dog was because I had never put my head in her lap? Was that possible? She knew I was a faggot. A couple of her brothers called me a fag at school. When I phoned her house and one of her brothers answered, I'd hear him saying, "It's your little fag boyfriend."

No way she was waiting for me to start something.

I was high, though. We were high as motherfuckers.

I heard myself in my stoned voice saying, "We should do it."

My just-having-inhaled-a-toke voice, pinched and squeaking.

"Why don't we—" I said, and she put a stop to that.

"What the fuck?" she said.

I was sort of insulted. "You think I can't do it?" I said. "Let's go get Greg's pot, and then drive to the Hackettstown Mall for a pack of broncos, and we can park in a cornfield near the Fairmont Church—"

"'Pack of broncos?'"

"I meant condoms."

"I know what you meant." She was really laughing now. "Are you high or something?"

I started laughing too, which killed the moment. I had a faggy laugh. I tossed my head back and opened my mouth and went, "Hah, hah, hah," and then my shoulders collapsed, and I was jelly in the front seat of Lottie's car. So was she. In Lottie's earnest German household, no one was silly. I was her fool. She liked to cue me, and she liked to *shush* me.

Shifting the car into gear, done laughing, she said, "Which way is Cindy's house?"

"I thought you got directions," I said, trying to decide if she had hurt my feelings. If my feelings should have been hurt. "I think we turn left up ahead."

She looked at me like she was about to say something she could never take back. Then changed her mind. "Try not to get wasted too fast," she said finally. "Okay? We have the whole night." Then she pulled away from the Stop sign and got to Cindy's house without my help.

✳ ✳ ✳

I was twenty-six years old before I told anyone about high school. I was ashamed. I knew I had caused it. The taunts, attacks, not daily but hourly threats, catcalls, public mocking, on the school bus, in hallways, like I said, in classrooms dissecting earthworms, on playing fields, in locker rooms, choir halls, in the auditorium when I was in school plays, in the lunchroom, the library, anywhere. For years afterward, I could not walk by a group of two or more people without wincing. Ready to be called a fag. I spent college waiting to be named.

It stopped when I moved to New York, where I could disappear. And I disappeared for half my twenties, into a blackout, not an alcoholic blackout but an emotional remove from my day, every day, for years.

Then I fell in love with a "healthcare professional." *Mental* health. We got in a fight once, I forget why. We fought a lot. It was a bad fight, and he hit me, hard across the face with his bare hand. He had been married—not gay-married, there wasn't gay marriage when he was in his twenties, or when I was in my twenties, or forties—and he wore a ring on the slapping hand. Maybe it was a wedding ring. Somehow I had never asked.

The ring left a scratch on my face. It was there for a while. I was more shocked than hurt. We were in his apartment, standing in the open door that led to a garden. It was August, hot and hazy, and the trees smelled like semen. Gingko trees. The smell of semen from flowering trees in the summer night.

My boyfriend was as handsome as he could possibly be, and older, which I liked. He was a man, another reason I liked him. I did not think of myself as a man.

He hit me really hard. I felt his ring scratching my face. He had been sexually abused as a child. He had been called a faggot by his father.

I cried, not from pain but surprise. Then I said, "They hated me." The words came out. They were not planned. We both heard them. "They hated me," I said, twenty times, a hundred times. I'm sure he had no idea what I was talking about. I stayed with him for six years. "They hated me, they hated me, they hated me." I was crying, and I couldn't stop. He was nice to me for a while afterward. "They hated me," I told him, just as stunned by the words as he was. My heart pumped them out of me, blood spurting with the force of a muscle contraction I couldn't control.

A mess I'd made that now I would have to clean up.

* * *

We parked behind a Peugeot in Cindy's circular drive and chased the sound of voices down a slate path that led to the back of the house. The path widened and became a patio around a pool whose surface sparkled with heat and reflected moonlight. "Jesus," Lottie said, either in warning or exclamation, or both. "Yeah, really," I said, staring at the pool, the patio, the curtained French doors thrown open to the lawn, and at the tanned girls in halter tops and peasant skirts lounging in iron chairs at the poolside, and the boys in shorts and polo shirts standing in the living room by the liquor cabinet, mixing drinks with sneaky names—Slow Comfortable Screw, Sex on the Beach—and playing Bob Dylan on the stereo.

At the edge of the patio, we stopped. I was careful to pause at the start of things. There was a chance I would giggle, or sing show tunes, or play with my hair. I had to remind myself to be cool. So far, none of the girls had seen us. Most of them were cheerleaders, like Cindy, and they could have been as far away as a football field they seemed so out of reach. Still, some of them were my friends.

I liked to hang out with girls because they were not afraid of anything. They were the real boys, lying, fearless, obscene, and indestructible. When they were not babysitting for their moms' friends, they cut class and drove drunk and made out in parked cars with boys so trashy even I could shun them. Or they crossed the Delaware River into Pennsylvania where they passed for legal in redneck bars and shot pool with bearded guys who lived in hippie communes out past Easton.

And they never got caught. Girls were shrewd. They were painful and impressive. Yet they made a show of their magnificence in order to attract—who? Jesus? Hollywood? Eternity? No, boys. The object of their charm and guts and rage was teenage boys.

Except Lottie. She didn't care about men, maybe because she had so many brothers. Cindy, in contrast, was all about guys. And the guys at her party were stalking out of the house, across the lawn, gleaming like open razors.

Ten, twelve guys. Who were they? Cindy had rounded up a bunch of Greg's pals for her cheerleader girlfriends. Preppy white boys from Princeton. Older, richer. Nineteen was older. They would have better pot and their own cars.

Strangers. Nobody I knew, which should have been a relief. A dozen guys who hadn't heard I was a fag. But that was almost worse. Because now I would have to watch them find out.

Wherever I went, within twenty miles of my high school, there might be someone who knew I was a fag. Word spread. I was unsafe in five counties, one of them in Pennsylvania. Whenever I walked into a store outside my high school district, through a suburban shopping mall, down the aisle of a movie theater in Flemington or Hackettstown, across the main street of a small town in Warren or Morris or Somerset or Mercer or Bucks County, or over a lawn spread with strangers at a friend's party a few miles from my parents' house, I did a quick count of how many people—if any—had already heard about me.

If one or two of them knew, they would tell everyone who didn't. If nobody knew, I was safe until somebody found out. Which someone always did. Because there was something about me. I gave myself away. Girls always knew but kept it to themselves, unless a boy they liked was around. Boys didn't always know, and it was terrifying to watch them figure it out.

The most dangerous place to be was where nobody knew until I did something overt. Which was—what? Mention Bobby Sherman? I was never sure what I'd done wrong. My only clue was in the way guys imitated me, mockingly, threateningly. They were my mirror. Did I swing my hips like they were doing? Dangle my wrists? Lisp? I knew I was a fag, I knew how I was a fag, knew the giveaway style of my faggotry, because of the boys who followed me around imitating fags.

My body gave me away. It always came out, whatever I couldn't control. And then I would have to watch a boy, or somebody's dad, who seemed to like me okay, wolf out on me like Frederick March face-melding from Dr. Jekyll into Mr. Hyde. The rage would spread across his face, and the guy who seconds ago was my friend—my friend for years, or my friend for minutes—drooled and spat and spun away and ran back to his buddies, to point and whisper and laugh, until they all turned to yell that I was a fag.

Faggot was their safe word. Their antidote. The threat I posed was viral. The rooms I infected, the lawn parties. I was a horror film. Tippi Hedren in *The Birds*, new girl in town, walks into a coffee shop where the locals cower in the corner, terrified of her love and trouble and the angry birds screeching in her wake. Was I a witch? *Carrie* was my autobiography. I saw it at the Hackettstown Mall. Sissy Spacek has the power to wreck a dance at the gym. Was I telekinetic? I could disfigure a face, turn nice guys into wolves. What made me such a faggot? I was asked that question every day.

Here was a lawn spread with boys who didn't know me and a dozen girls who did. Sometimes the girls could be trusted not to say what I was. Maybe this time . . .

Then Cindy came out, laughing and holding hands with a guy. Was that Greg? Princeton boy? Lottie's dealer? He was tall as somebody's dad. Cindy was four foot nine, if that. Barefoot in blue jeans and a black hooded blouse, she came up to Greg's bent elbow as he lifted her hand to his lips and kissed the back of her palm.

He was wearing khaki shorts, burgundy penny loafers with no socks, and a pink Oxford cloth button-down shirt, untucked and hanging over his ass.

The boys who sold pot to Lottie didn't wear pink shirts. They were from Teaneck, and they had peach fuzz on their pimpled cheeks and Jethro Tull on their tape decks.

Slouching, pink-clad, with an air of elitism that was nothing like the jock boy smugness of the guys in my high school, and with brown hair that hung to his shoulders but not in a girly way, like mine, Greg delivered Cindy to her guests.

That was their conceit, that the party was Cindy's debut. And she made an impression. She was not flamboyant; she was just buoyant. With her black hair newly bowl-cut like Dorothy Hamill's, she looked cute and happy and half his height, yet he leaned down to her effortlessly, and she seemed to float into his grasp.

Everyone had stopped talking in order to watch Greg lean and Cindy float. Lottie and I got a tracking shot of the action. Then the two of them turned and headed for us, for Lottie and me. Nervously, I grabbed Lottie's hand and squeezed it hard. It was the first time we had held hands. Except for passing a joint, we hardly ever touched.

"Look," I said. "It's the Great Gatsby."

She didn't seem to care that I was clutching her palm. Or, no, she was pretending not to notice. I felt her indifference. Wow, that was new. I was startled. "Are you pissed at me?" I said. "Because I asked about sex? I was kidding."

"Oh, Jesus."

"You're pissed because I'm not Jesus? You're tired of driving? I'm sorry I don't have my license. I'm sorry you have to drive while I'm getting high."

"I have to drive while *I'm* getting high."

"And I'm sorry for that."

"I really don't know what you're talking about," she said.

I was being dismissed in favor of him. That guy. Lottie was my armor, and I could not afford to lose her to a boy. Even worse, he was dressed fruity, and I was supposed to be the queer. If I had to be a faggot, then I was going to be *the* faggot. I'm not calling him a homo. Maybe he was French, or southern, or Episcopalian. I didn't care what he was. For now, I wanted Lottie's attention to be centered, again and as always, on me. I was ready to bug her if that was the only way to keep her.

"Did I say something stupid at dinner?" I asked.

"You didn't say anything at dinner."

"I don't like to speak in your house. I'm afraid of your dad."

"Everyone's afraid of my dad. He's the chief of police."

"Why are you repeating everything I say?"

"Who said I was repeating everything you say?"

"I did. Do you want me to go? You're my ride. If I leave, you have to take me."

"Shh," she said, stage manager during a scene change. After all, I was her stage crew. During *My Fair Lady*, she taught me to wear black and fade into the background. If I had been visible onstage while the lights were dimmed and the audience was breathing, it would wreck things.

She was a great teacher, funny and smart, and just mean enough to make you want to do things her way. And always there was her gravelly, melodic laugh. Maybe my small rage at Greg was a student's possessive love for his teacher. I wanted to be her only pupil.

I knew I was overreacting. But I felt like I was watching the end of our friendship glide across the lawn.

When Greg and Cindy finally reached us, their arrival coincided with a special effect: the porch lights on the side of the house went dark, and a dozen lights inlaid around the ledge of the pool flashed on. Steam rose from the water, and everyone clapped. Cindy introduced the two of us to Greg, who said nothing. Oh, he had that silent grace, like all authentic guys. It didn't matter if they were chicken farmers or bankers' sons, boys knew how to be quiet and still. I was irritated by his calm, and I pulled Lottie's hand to my lips, mockingly, as if for a kiss. I would have licked her palm if she hadn't stopped me.

"What the hell is wrong with you?" she said.

Cindy was nodding. In agreement? She was another friend from high school musicals. Last April, our spring musical was *The Fantasticks*, and I was the Boy, and Cindy was the Wall, a mute part. She ran around in black tights, handing out props and dropping tinfoil rain on me and the Girl. When her back was turned to the audience, she made goofy faces, mocking our love scenes—just to be silly, not mean.

In real life, she was not satirical. She was a cheerleader. She was also the only Asian American student in my 99 percent white high school, and so small she was always the girl who got hoisted to the top of the human pyramid the cheerleaders built at pep rallies and homecoming games. "I'm tiny and Korean," she said, in the tone of blunt realism that was her adjustment to being surrounded and alone. "Where else would they put me? Up there for everyone to stare at. Trapped, but on top!"

She was matter-of-fact. And she was matter-of-factly laughing as she held hands with Greg. "We're all friends," she said. "Okay?" It was a cheerleader's *Okay!* It meant the game was on, and the game was, "Don't sell pot in the middle of my backyard. Be cool." Everyone was gravely silent. Marijuana was the most serious thing we could think of. We smoked cheap weed in parked cars and cemeteries in the dark, but we acted like we were outlaw dealers hiding from both a drug cartel and the FBI.

Then Greg cleared his throat.

That was all—but for a minute, nobody moved or made a sound. He was standing in the middle of the circle we had formed around him, sulking prettily like a boy who resents the attention that he demands you give him.

I saw how foolish I had been to suggest sex to Lottie. To plead. Desire was coaxed forth not by entreaty but disdain, and Greg was both needy and aloof, with a sexy stoop to his shoulders and a lazy patrician frown.

Lottie, who was never weird around guys, was looking away from him so intently that it was a declaration of love. Cindy was airborne, an actress raised to the rafters to play Peter Pan.

I wanted a cigarette. That would be a mistake. I smoked wrong. Guys smoked like they were taking a lonely shit after a losing game, straining against their rage and constipation: brief stabbing drags, the cigarette gripped between their thumb and pointer finger and driven into their mouths. What fun was that? Smoking was supposed to be graceful, elaborate, British. I was afraid to light up in front of Greg because he would find out I smoked with an accent. What's more, I was staring at his chest, at the span of collarbone visible at the base of his neck. He must have thought I was looking at the menthols in the pocket over his heart because he fished out the pack and held it flat in his palm, saying, "Want one?"

I pictured Lottie's dad offering cake to Caesar, and I thought, "Now I'm the dog."

"You don't smoke menthol," Cindy said. She told Greg. "He doesn't smoke menthols."

"He smokes OPs," Lottie said, maybe trying to insult me. "Other People's."

Were they about to tell Greg that I was a fag? I trusted them. They wouldn't betray me. Talking about me in the third person was as far as they would go. How far would I go? Greg's presence was disorienting. His body. A rip in the fabric where the story begins, threads unraveling. No one could be trusted when a cute boy was around.

Then again, he spoke.

"Go ahead," he said, holding out his cigarettes. "Help yourself."

"Sure, thanks," I said, shrugging like it was no big deal, either way.

I was lying, of course.

It was a really big deal.

Because yikes.

I was a gay faggot.

I had never seen anyone as beautiful as Greg.

✱ ✱ ✱

I wasn't gay, I was a girl.

Not just a girl. I was an actress. I yearned to be. I still do. I wanted especially to be an actress in 1970s Hollywood movies. Those women! They were so much better than men. Unlike men, they showed their need. They were porous with need, and yet, paradoxically, needed hardly anything at all. You're Streisand, you're Liza, what else could you possibly need?

Jane Fonda, Jill Clayburgh, Ellen Burstyn. Barbara Harris, Cicely Tyson, Carrie Snodgress, Cloris Leachman, Shelley Duvall. Sissy Spacek, Diahann Carroll, Karen Black. Miss Diana Ross as Billie Holiday: two miracles at once. The expression on Lily Tomlin's face as she watches Keith Carradine sing "I'm Easy" in *Nashville*! Their strength was in putting themselves at risk. They reached out. Protecting everyone but themselves. Protecting themselves by refusing protection. They gave whatever they had and seemed to be safest with nothing. Deprivation as strength. It was a dangerous lesson: strength lay in giving yourself away.

They wanted connection. What did the men want? Paul Newman wanted beer. Warren Beatty wanted someone else's wife. Robert Redford wanted Newman. They didn't want you. They gave nothing and then disappeared. Why want them? Yet the camera did. When the men came in the room, everything stopped. The women stopped, the camera stopped to stare with pained apprehension at the men, who would either fuck you, or ignore you, or refuse to fuck you, or fuck you and ignore you. Fucking was ignoring, it was a way to erase you.

How I wanted to be Jane Fonda when I was twelve. I was in love with her self-consciousness. There was a space between her performance and herself. She didn't consume her characters like Bette Davis devouring every part she played. Jane Fonda left a window open between her privacy and her sense of being seen. She knew who was watching: her directors and photographers, all men, with their penis cameras.

I wanted her power to survive their gaze.

The boys who called me "faggot" didn't try to photograph or fuck me. I wasn't being sexually exploited or displayed. But they threatened me, humiliated me, day after day.

If I could be Jane Fonda. If I could be Jodie Foster in *Taxi Driver*. She was fourteen, nearly my age, playing a prostitute. Was that a viable career option? For me, I mean? Could I at least get boys to *pay* to abuse me? They shoved their swollen, blood-engorged heads in my face, and called me a "fucking faggot," and splattered me with rage.

✱ ✱ ✱

Cindy's party was nearly done. No one was left. Just the four of us: me, Lottie, Cindy, and Greg. It was the fag end of the night. That's what I kept saying. Out loud.

"It's the fag end of the night!"

I was sitting by the pool, wasted. We all were. For the past couple hours, Greg had been tending bar, where he mixed highballs from the Prohibition era—Monkey Glands and Sidecars and Luigis. Who knew what they were? Cindy tried them all. Before now, her history of lifetime drinking had been limited to things that went with Coke: rum and Coke, Jack and Coke, 7 and 7 with Coke instead of 7-Up. It wasn't long before she got sick on Greg's bartending, and while she ran off to puke, most of her guests left. She hardly noticed their absence when she came back out to the patio and sank into a chaise longue. It was made of cast iron and fitted with a long blue pillow, and Cindy collapsed across it.

Lottie didn't like to drink—"The only thing that doesn't make me barf on contact is tequila," she said—and no matter how much pot she smoked, she never seemed high.

Sober, expectant, she lay on the diving board, stretched out on her belly, her chin propped on her crossed arms. I don't know when or how she got up there. Had she made her drug deal with Greg? They had hardly spoken to each other from the second they met.

No one talked. We seemed to have slept, and when we opened our eyes to look around, and to anchor ourselves to the conscious world, here was our evidence of situation and self: Lottie tensile and vibrant on the diving board, Cindy merging with the lawn furniture, and Greg and me facing each other across the pool.

Four of us squared off around a rectangle. A wrecked tangle: I was high and punning. Cindy was drunk and burbling. Greg was sipping at one of his cocktails. Both Lottie and I were secretly watching him, though Lottie's secret was much more open. At the tip of the diving board, her head slightly bounced, the pinspots of her round glasses flickering up and down Greg's body.

He had taken off his pink shirt and burgundy shoes and, in his white V-neck T-shirt and khaki shorts, he sat by the edge of the pool, soaking his feet in the water and his face in the moonlight. His brown hair spilled from his head and ended at the crest of collarbone where his T-shirt left a pale line of flesh before exposing the ripe burn of his suntanned skin.

I never felt the dislocating pain of desire until I saw Greg. Before he showed up at Cindy's pool, I was undifferentiated from whatever I touched or saw, as if everything were me, including not just Lottie but her mom's cake, and her dad's dog, and her hippie car. Greg flung me out in the world. I mean, my dick got hard. What was I supposed to do about that?

Cindy was high as a motherfucker, and Lottie was watching Greg, our James Taylor, pretty white boy with long brown hair. Would he find a guitar and sing "Fire and Rain"? Which of us would he pick? I had to speak up. I had no idea what it would take to get someone other than me involved with my stiff dick, but if I was a gay faggot, maybe this was the time to say so. I couldn't quite, though. What I managed instead was this:

"Lottie says Jesus is a dog."

I was betraying her in my clumsy way. Was she about to betray me with Greg? It was worse to want boys than to fear them.

I tried to catch Lottie's eye, to see if she'd heard what I said. But she was still watching Greg. Before I knew what I was doing, I was talking so loudly that even Cindy grunted.

"She thinks Jesus is a German Shepherd," I said. "Named Caesar."

I turned my head back and forth, watching Lottie and Greg, tracking their response, which they expressed by growing even more immobile. In the background was Bob Dylan's "Blood on the Tracks," which drifted outside from the living room through open French doors hung with sheer drapes that blew in the breeze.

Dylan was singing "Shelter from the Storm," about form and void and wilderness.

"Jesus eats from the table, without utensils," I said.

"Me too," Cindy said. Did she know what she was saying? It hardly mattered. Like the rest of us, she was waiting. We were all filled with waiting, or rather, with waiting for the wait to be done: the wait for whatever we wanted or hated to happen, for Greg to choose or Lottie to speak, for Cindy to wake or sleep, for me to be gay.

Then Lottie stood. Swaying at the end of the diving board, she took off her shoes and shirt, her jeans and bra, her panties, and her socks, balancing expertly, partly on one leg. She put her eyeglasses on top of her clothes. And then she jumped blind and naked into the pool.

It was maybe the most selfish thing she had ever done. As in, calling attention solely to herself. She swam a lap across the pool and back. She was a good swimmer.

Greg laughed, put down his drink, stood up, and undressed. Then he, too, jumped in the pool. I watched this naked guy swim with my friend. The water distorted their bodies, so they looked wavy and green. They reached the shallow end and pulled themselves onto the blue lip of the tiled pool.

Clearly, Lottie wasn't me. She was not embarrassed about being naked, but she was not showing off. In her nakedness, it was only her hands that seemed exposed, and I wanted to cover them with mine.

Greg was surprisingly soft. Nothing like the guys in my gym class, farmers' sons and football stars. Greg had a preppy white boy's pale soft body. When he leaned back and lay flat at the side of the pool with his feet still in the water, his chest and hips and thighs were a straight line, his gut scooped, and the bones of his pelvis were sharp.

It was his pelvic bones that made me stop breathing. I mean the depression between his groin and the jutting, saber-edged bone of the furthest edge of his hip.

Everyone was brightly lit in the pool lights. We were instantly no longer high. Lottie was staring straight ahead. Greg had an erection. I had never seen an erect penis before. Just mine. Greg's curved, which shocked me. Another shock: as he put his arm around Lottie, he was looking at me. Directly. It lasted a few seconds, but he made sure I saw. Then he closed his eyes and buried his face in her neck.

* * *

Girls were better than boys.

Lit in everyone's gaze, surviving it, or fighting it, or using it, or liking it, or ignoring it. Not even noticing it.

Girls named Trudy, and Sharon, and Cathy, and Kathleen, and Karen, and Mary Ann, and Donna, and Laurie, and Maureen.

White girls. It was rural Northwestern New Jersey. There was one African-American girl in our grade school, and there were three Jewish girls, two of them sisters. My best girlfriend in the fourth grade was Japanese and Jewish. She moved away. My sixth-grade girlfriend was Puerto Rican. No one else was. For the Christmas swap, she bought me an ID bracelet inscribed with her name.

They were girls, but I was worse than a girl because I wasn't a girl. I wasn't supposed to be a girl.

First-grade girls who played jump rope at the bottom of the field behind the building and let me play, and chanted while I jumped. "A rich man, a poor man, a beggar man, a thief—"

Sixth-grade girls who got suspended because they wore pantsuits, and girls were not allowed to wear pants, not even polyester.

Eighth-grade girls who kissed each other playing spin-the-bottle at birthday parties because the guests were twelve girls and me.

Some of them must have been gay. I hope they were gay. Some of them were boys. I hope they're still boys. They were kinder, gentler boys. They made more believable boys.

Girls who got perfect scores on standardized tests. Who jumped naked from diving boards. Who smelled like horse liniment. Who raised goats. Who ironed their hair. Who showed me how to braid my wet hair at night with rubber bands and wake in the morning with frizz that hung to my shoulders.

I hope I don't sound like a Billy Joel song.

Girls who mocked you for liking Billy Joel songs.

Who called me "faggot" sometimes when boys were around.

Who never called me a faggot when boys weren't around, which was one way I knew the difference between girls and boys.

Catholic girls who went to church on Saturday nights.

Homecoming queens in puffy dresses bending down to dance with boys.

Girls who read Langston Hughes and Sylvia Plath. Who wrote poetry they stole from Neil Young.

Who wrote me letters that they folded small and tied in knots. Knot notes; I have them in a drawer somewhere.

Who waited tables and served ice cream sundaes and saved their money to get out of there.

Girls who took me to movies in their father's car.

Who held my hand.

Girls playing clarinet in marching band, or twirling batons, or running track, or dissecting frogs while I turned the color of frogs.

Who played Cat Stevens and Stevie Wonder on their stereos and burned watermelon incense in glazed incense burners shaped like elephants and sang Carole King songs.

Girls who did what they wanted and knew you watched. Or did

what you wanted, because they knew they were watched. Or never thought about what anyone watched.

Girls who fell in love with each other. Or themselves! Who fell in love with boys, like I did.

✳ ✳ ✳

The day of high school graduation, I missed the school bus. I was stuck. There was no question of heading back to my parents' house, waking my brother, begging a ride. He had already fetched me from Cindy's place in the middle of the night. So I started to walk. The high school was seven miles off, and I got nearly halfway there, down to Route 31, when Lottie appeared.

"Hey, you," she said.

She had driven onto the shoulder of the road, and she was leaning out of her car, calling my name.

It was like the end of *The Fantasticks*, where the Boy comes back to the Girl after a long time away and sings about how everything he ever saw was her. Except we weren't singing. And no one had been gone long. What's more, I was the pining girl, and she was the rambling man, though I didn't expect a song on her return. I was half hoping she had Greg in the car.

"You, kid," she yelled.

The driver door swung open as she pulled alongside me. She was alone. I could see that she had not been home last night. Her hair was both frizzy and lank, uncombed, tangled and stiff where the chlorine had dried it out.

"Come on," she said.

She drove slowly beside me on the shoulder of the road. It was awkward for her, which made me happy.

"Ask me how I got home last night after you went off with him," I said. Cars sped by, north and south, blasting us with tail wind.

"You freak," she said.

"That's what my brother said when I woke him to come get me. He said some other stuff, too."

"Come on," she said, so roughly I could tell she was worried.

I really wanted to get in her car.

"I like walking," I said. I was a few feet ahead of her now, and she was inching along behind. We moved like this down the side of the road, sweating in the June heat. Cars honked, thinking we were idiots. I loved her following me.

"Hey, you," Lottie said. "Put your ass in my damned car."

I had mocked her in public, and she had left me by the side of the pool with a swollen dick and no ride home. Which one of us was more hurt? I hoped it was me. Could I afford to sulk? No. I wanted Lottie back. I wanted her to get out of her car and come for me. I stopped walking and stood still. Lottie killed the engine. I waited for her by the side of the road.

What is the thrill of knowing without looking that someone you love has come up beside you? I loved her. It wasn't the same way I yearned for Greg, but so what? Stupid boy. It hurt to look at him. Lottie was different. I knew the shape of her by my side. Her shoulders and arms. I heard the rasp of her breath.

"Fuck you," she said, real praise.

"I'd rather walk."

We were talking the way we always did. It would be okay. Six months or a year from now, when there was time, we could ask each other what happened. Meanwhile, I got out a cigarette that I had stolen from my mom. "Got a light?"

She reached in her jeans pocket for a pack of matches. "Stand close," she said, pulling us inside the shelter of the car door to block the wind. We crouched, and she struck a match. The first one didn't catch.

"Shit," she said.

There was a red bruise on her bare neck. Scratch marks, like a cat's. I touched it, and she frowned.

"Don't," she said.

"You look terrible," I said.

"I slept in my car."

"With him?"

"Shut up," she said.

"You let him, didn't you?"

She struck another match, which caught. For a while, we smoked, saying nothing. Smoking was tragic. I wanted every cigarette to taste like the first drag I ever took when I was twelve years old, the harsh, surprising warmth stinging the inside of my mouth. It never happened. I kept smoking because I hoped it would be like it had been. Smoking was nostalgia for smoking.

We finished our cigarettes. Then she produced a treat: two joints. My present. Greg's Colombian. She had scored in every sense, apparently. "Happy Graduation to You," she mock-sang, handing me the joints.

"I don't think I need these," I said. "I'm pretty burnt out from last night."

"Hair of the dog."

"Which dog? Caesar? Jesus? Greg?"

She smacked at me. "Get in the fucking car," she said.

So I did. I couldn't think what else to do. "Where do we go now?" I said.

We sat in the car getting high, staring blankly at New Jersey.

Then, out of the blue, she said, "He kisses like a boy." We were taking hits off a shared joint. "What does that mean?" I said. "'Like a boy?'" This was new information: Lottie knew how boys kissed. Not just Greg. She had been kissing boys. "Like the way boys do it," she said, shrugging. She looked like Diane Keaton with her blonde hair and her long straight nose. I realized suddenly that she was wearing Greg's white V-neck T-shirt. It looked good on her. I wondered what he'd gone home wearing. "He does it with just the tip of his tongue," she said. "I guess he thinks it's his 'move.' Just the tip. It's like kissing a guitar pick. Sorry," she said. "You wouldn't know about that."

"Maybe I would," I said, possibly out loud.

And then, still holding the lit joint, she grabbed the back of my neck with her right hand and pulled me forward, guiding a pet. And she kissed me. Wearing Greg's shirt. She still had smoke in her lungs, which she exhaled into my mouth. That was our story, if anyone asked. She was shotgunning me, in farewell. Normally it was done with the burning joint in somebody's lips, but not this time. Our teeth made a scraping sound. She held me there for a minute. Then she let go of my neck.

I shook my head like a dog. I think I heard my ears flap. When we separated, we were both blinking, as if we had just stood for a portrait in front of one of those cameras with giant flashbulbs that went off with a brilliant flash and a puff of smoke. I took her hand as she dropped it from my shoulders. I wasn't looking at her. Across the highway, in a cleared cornfield, were three new half-built houses, raw and pink in the morning sun. I stared at them, holding on to her hand. Then I let go, and she started the car and drove me to school.

✳ ✳ ✳

When did I see her last?

Just before my graduation ceremony, in the hallway near the cafeteria, she made me spin once in my cap and gown. She set my mortarboard at an angle on my head. I watched her push her glasses up on her nose. Then I lost sight of her. She spun out of range behind me as I went to join my classmates.

Was she at the ceremony? Did she stay to watch? I never saw her again, after that afternoon, and for ten years I never talked about my high school graduation with anyone, and no one ever asked.

* * *

After their naked swim, Lottie and Greg had disappeared. I wasn't clear about the chain of events. Just that I had been left behind with Cindy, who was passed out, an elastic string of drool hanging from her lips as she lay on her chaise longue. Horseflies were dive-bombing her arms and legs, leaving welts that swelled up from her exposed flesh. I carried her into the house and settled her on the linen couch. While I was in the living room, I called my brother to come get me. Then I sat by the pool and finished Greg's drink. It was foamy and warm. I didn't like whiskey. But it had been Greg's.

"This is it," I said, not exactly to myself.

I lit a cigarette and waved my arm around, gesturing, theatrical, British. I tried to notice where my skin stopped and the air began. What if everything was not me? What would that be like? My flesh stung like I'd been swarmed by Cindy's flies. It wasn't the worst feeling. I pictured Greg in Lottie's car. He'd be leaning back in my seat. Or maybe she had let him drive. Which one of them did I hate more? Neither, both. Neither one of them was me.

I thought about the people I wasn't. About what was going to happen at graduation tomorrow. Then I took off my clothes, jumped in the pool, and swam a lap. Afterward, I stretched out in the grass. God, I hated my body, having and being a body. It trapped me, exposed me, betrayed me. Embarrassed me. It was me.

I was still lying naked on the lawn an hour later when my brother showed up.

Scenes from a Marriage

The second to the last time he gets out of the hospital, the last time being his death, Dave goes on a farewell tour, like Cher. He has just published his new book. His third, his last. It's an account of the final year of his life, and it's impossible to read—partly because I'm in it, doing nothing to keep him alive, and partly because he won't stop joking about what hurts most. "My T-cell count is lower than my IQ," he writes. "If I were Dan Quayle, I'd be dead now."

Two weeks before he dies, his publisher sends him thirty copies of the book, and I load Dave and his books into a cab, and we drive around town handing them out to every agent or editor or cute boy who's ever rejected him.

He is also trying to get someone to publish the diary he kept while he was in the hospital. It's a black Mead Composition notebook, and it's an aborted novel, a toilet joke, an archive of AIDS obituaries from the *New York Times* for September and half of October 1994, a list of results of blood tests, CAT scans, MRIs, bone marrow tests, colonoscopies, and bronchoscopies, a document of rage, and a draft of Top Ten Lists—Top Ten Most Embarrassing Public Bowel Movements, Top Ten Cutest Male Nurses.

And it's an autobiography in the form of a questionnaire. There are five hundred questions, which Dave has written in block letters in his careful third-grader's print:

1. Name: _____

2. Age: _____

3. Religious Persuasion: _____

4. Number of lifetime sexual partners (in thousands) (circle one):

        0–10   10–20   A Lady Doesn't Tell

5. Life expectancy: _____

And so on, for pages. He has supplied answers. They're scribbled in his barely readable cursive script. His name is "Legion." His age is "You should die like this, you'd know what aging is." For "Religious Persuasion," he has written "Liza." He doesn't answer the question about sexual partners. Next to "Life Expectancy," he writes, "I've got ten minutes to live, but who's counting? Now I've got nine."

We take this diary to several literary agents. David already has an agent, but he fired him because he brought ice cream to the hospital room. "Ice cream, for God's sake!" Dave screamed. "Ice cream is dairy! Dairy goes right through me! If I had lung cancer, would you bring me a pack of Virginia Slims?"

We visit Charlotte Sheedy, Audre Lorde's agent. She's also Ally Sheedy's mom. "In the future, I won't work with anyone who hasn't repped a Black Lesbian and raised a movie star," Dave says when our cab pulls up to her building on lower Broadway. Then, "Fuck you," he says, for no reason. He is always meanest in cabs. I'm getting money out of my pocket. I've been broke my whole adult life, but I took a steady job just as Dave started getting sick, and for the first time in our friendship, I can pay for things. Lately, I'm paying all the time.

Which: fine. He has always paid for me, bought lunch, taken me to Broadway shows, orchestra seats, shelled out a cash loan for a month's rent, several times. I'm happy to pay. Relieved. I can't keep him alive, but I can pay.

He, though, hates the shift in power. Paying is his job, his privilege. It's his way, he jokes, of making people love him.

"Don't overtip," he screams as we're leaving the cab. "Jesus. Get a receipt. Do you think you're a Rockefeller? You're not. Guess why? Guess
why you're not a Rockefeller? Rockefellers have money because they
don't tip and they *save their receipts.*"

We climb from the cab. He weighs ninety-seven pounds. So he
walks slowly. His death walk, all bones. The skin at the back of his neck
is creased and dry, sinewy. His hair is pin-straight, slicked against his
skull. One arm goes out to the side for balance. The other ends in a fist
that clutches the waistband of his jeans.

His pants are a sight gag. Let go, and they fall. He knows this, and
he'll drop them to shock you. He leaves his zipper open to show his diapers. The pants and diapers are white, and so is his T-shirt, which is
scrunched up over the Hickman catheter spliced to his chest above his
right nipple. His down coat is a blue pall. He'd scold me for that line.
"'Blue pall!' Miss Thing! What is it, poetry month?" And he'd laugh his
three-syllable laugh, "Hant, hant, hant."

He's a little diapered man in a blue shroud, holding his pants up
and moving stiffly and delicately across the sidewalk. He is thirty-eight
years old.

Now we're pushing through the door to Charlotte Sheedy's office,
and there is the surprised assistant at her guard post. She stands up,
then darts back, freaked out by what flew in. AIDS is good for something, a way to get access to anybody, push past office lackeys. Waving
his hand, Dave says, "We have an appointment," and we keep walking, through the door to the inner sanctuary, straight to Charlotte
Sheedy's desk.

Dave sits in a wooden chair. Sits, slides. The chair's slippery, or he
is, or both. Or the problem is his coat. It's a sled, and he rides it down
off the chair seat until he's sitting on his neck. Then he pulls himself
up. Again. And Again. "Such a little figure / slipped quiet from its
chair": Emily Dickinson. It's on my mind. Did I say it out loud? More
poetry, my response to loss. Don't help, just recite. Dave hates me

because I can't help. Or I can, only a little bit, and right now. Dying is a series of instant victories over nothing immediately fatal in preparation for complete loss. Will he not die if I find the right poem? If I can separate him from his coat? Let's pretend I can save him from his coat, at least. Our lie agreed upon. I get him out of the thing, which he drapes over the arm of his chair, and sits still.

Now he's a pair of shoulder blades in a T-shirt, and above them, a face. Huge head, shrunken body. His glasses are Dr. Eckleberg's, a billboard that stares at you. There's a narcissistic boon in watching David die because he lights on you with an urgency and directness that no one else has ever spent. His gaze. Sure, it indicts you, dictates and controls, but you're hot and lit, a movie star in your key light.

Floodlights on Charlotte Sheedy, who has been sitting behind her desk and watching calmly, waiting for the best moment to speak.

"Oh, Charlotte Sheedy," Dave says. His voice is high and loud and raspy and sweet. "I have brought you my *new* book, and also my *newest* book."

I'm standing behind him. He's a film director, and I'm his people. He raises his right hand, signaling me, and I step forward and hand Sheedy his two manuscripts—the new book and the hospital diary.

"I want you," he tells her, pausing to haul himself higher in his chair, and to catch his breath, and to grab his pants, which have not moved up the chair with the rest of him, "to represent me. From now on."

Charlotte Sheedy is spectacularly cool. She opens Dave's new book, the published one, congratulates him, thumbs through a few pages, and then sets it aside with a palm flat on its cover, both stamping it with her approval and absorbing its contents through her fingertips in an apparent flash of superhuman appraisal. Then she takes up Dave's diary, which, in her hands, is not a receptacle of rage and rubber hospital gloves and blue pills stapled and glued to lined notebook pages, but an ordinary book proposal. She is so smooth, I want her to be my agent too, possibly my mom.

One page of the diary is entirely black, and she stops there. Dave inked it solid with a magic marker one hospital afternoon, frowning while he told me that he hoped he didn't go to hell because he was tired of running into me. "Even in hell," he said, "I'd have to buy you lunch."

She stares at the page and says, "I see." Then she closes the book, looks up.

Our eyes meet over Dave's head. I am trying to make my face say, "Sorry, sorry, sorry." Charlotte Sheedy is nicer than I am, though. She doesn't collude with me in silent commentary about a man who is clearly at the end of his life.

Instead, she looks at Dave. "I'm not sure this is ready to be shown around," she says. Maybe she gets sick writers in her office all the time. Maybe all writers are ten minutes from death. "Please keep me in mind, though," she says, "when you have something that's finished."

Dave grins, showing all his teeth. "Darling," he says. "I completely agree." He stands slowly and heads around her desk for a hug. They meet by her chair and do a quick theatrical cheek-to-cheek air kiss.

And then we're listening to Dave breathe.

His fierce breaths.

It's an effort for him to stand up. I haven't dared to help him because there's nothing wrong! That's the story he's telling. He's not a man with just days to live; he's a potential client with a literary property he's shopping around.

And what am I, then? His people; his amanuensis; development girl; his chauffeur; his "longtime companion," nonsexual; his stock boy, carting books; his pocket change; hailer of cabs; his walker, as if he were a woman in fur on the Upper East Side. His George Hamilton, accompanying Lynda Bird Johnson, the President's daughter, to the Academy Awards, which Hamilton did in 1966, in white tie and a spray tan. Dave would get that reference. He loves anything tacky and obscure. He loves failed and minor stars. Three months ago, it would have made him laugh.

Now, though. He's going to die, and all I have is George Hamilton with a fake tan.

Dave is breathing in Charlotte Sheedy's office. We're all breathing. She breathes, I breathe, we listen to Dave breathe. We count the breaths, which come slowly, with labor. Breath, pause. Breath, pause. We stand there, waiting for what's next.

* * *

I'm with Dave on the futon couch in his living room in Chelsea. He's decided to throw a theme party—"I'm Still Standing," which is a lie— and I'm addressing invites that need to be out fast because the party's a week away, and he doesn't want to die before anyone can RSVP.

I'm writing names on envelopes. He's doing an eight-hour IV drip. Pentamidine, a prophylactic against pneumonia. A guy named Pepper, healthcare professional, has come with equipment: IV bag, rolling stand, yards of clear tubing, and a hypodermic needle. Pepper is a straight guy with a tattoo on his left arm. He sets up the IV in the corner near the window. The fat bag hangs on its silver pole, and Pepper unwinds several feet of tubing, which he hooks to the needle. Then he smacks Dave's arm to find a vein.

"You're not slapping me again unless we have a safe word," Dave says.

Pepper laughs. He's wearing rubber gloves, blue jeans, and a sleeveless T-shirt. "What a fabulous tattoo," Dave says. He's right; it's awesome. It stretches from Pepper's shoulder to his elbow, curving around his bicep, and it shows a military grunt in battle fatigues cradling his wounded buddy in his outstretched arms.

An all-male *Pietà* in blue and gold, framed by swirls.

"I have an outfit that color," Dave says.

I'm reading the tattoo like it's about me. *Pietà*: I'm Mary with her wounded son in her cradling arms. Or switch roles, and I'm Jesus, crucified by what I've been sent to save. No wonder David yells at me. My Christ thing. Closet Catholic. When Dave told me he had AIDS, the day we met, I liked him more. Creepy fetish, dying men. Except it was 1989 in NYC, and the chances of meeting someone who didn't have AIDS, in that place and time, were—forgive the word—slim. And I hadn't kept anyone else alive. Maybe Dave. If he had five years, surely there'd be a cure . . .

He had five years, in any case.

Now he's dying, and I'm jealous. I'm competitive with Dave's death. It's all he cares about: dying, not dying. I want him to care that he's losing me. I know how selfish that sounds. I never say it to him. Death doesn't just shroud, it also snaps the sheet back, and you get to see how your best beloved looks naked and stripped of flesh and left a bone clutter in a sack of skin, sometimes smeared with shit. That's what a body is and does. You see him, and yourself: you're a sniveling want machine, saying, "Stop that. Don't die. Talk to me."

I have to outwit my rival, Dave's death. So when Pepper pinches Dave's skin and pierces it, digging the needle into the green-veined underside of Dave's wrist, I force myself to watch. Needles make me sick, but I want David to know I'm not afraid. I'm better than death. I can handle whatever happens to his body. I must be turning pale with nausea, though, because he screams.

"Stop staring," he screams.

I'm sitting next to him, holding a ballpoint pen, my lap a writing board. There is a half-addressed envelope on my thigh.

Pepper is tracking the flow of viscous fluid through the tube into David's wrist.

"Stop looking at me like nothing human could ever offend you," Dave says.

"I'm sorry," I say, putting the pen down.

"I *want* you to be offended."

"I wasn't trying to upset you."

"Of *course* you were trying to upset me. You want my attention." He splits "attention" into its three parts: uh—TEN—shun. "How brave you are. How caring. I've got news for you. You're not the Messiah. You're a fag. I'm a *dying* fag. I win the Suffering Sweepstakes. You think this is happening to *you*. Well, it's not. Look," Dave shouts, holding up his pierced wrist. "Me," he says, showing me his wrist, which he waves in the air.

The needle pulls at his skin. Pepper leaps forward. Dave ignores him and points at me.

"You," he says.

He moves his hand back to his chest. The needle's tearing at his skin, and there's blood. He hits his chest.

"Me," he repeats.

"You need to chill," Pepper tells him.

"Go fuck yourself," David says.

✳ ✳ ✳

A week later, Dave's Chelsea living room is packed with queers and a few straight women, ten days before he dies. Everyone is standing; only David is sitting. It's impossible to find him unless you glance down, which is hard because people are shoulder to shoulder. Dave's at knee level. He's been taking Haldol for anxiety, and he's doped up and zoned out, nesting in a corner of his futon couch like a small brown hoot owl.

People ask me, What's up, where's Dave? I'll show you, I say. Then I guide them to the couch. Dave, I say. His chin is on his chest. Slowly, he looks up.

"Someone to see you," I say.

"Oh, darling," he says, stretching out his hand, which is blue with puncture marks from IV drips. "It's been such hell."

He's known for his theme parties, which are famously bad.

My first was his David Party. Five years ago, in his old place in Hell's Kitchen. He said all gay men in New York were named Christopher or Stephen—"Full names! With a *ph*! No gay man is ever just 'Steve!'"—and he invited thirty *David*s to his cattle chute apartment in a four-floor walk-up on 9th Avenue. A cramped and airless studio facing the street. You could stand in the middle with your arms spread and touch both walls. It opened off the second-floor landing and ran straight back to a foldout couch under a window that was closed tight against the fire escape.

He sent invites to David Bowie, David Geffen, and David Letterman. "I couldn't believe Letterman was in the phone book!" He made name tags—"Hello, My Name Is: David"—and served David's Cookies. On his TV, he showed a video with the sound turned down: Richard Gere in *King David*.

I called from the corner payphone on Fifty-Second Street. "Can I speak to David?" A few minutes later, I showed up at his door. "You can't come in," he said, "because I'm expecting—"

"I get it," I said.

He let me stay. Mute gay men stood against the walls, holding drinks. He had invited twenty men who'd never met each other. Twenty strange Davids. No one moved or spoke. It was a gay bar on Friday night before anyone was drunk. "Let me do introductions," David said, leading me around. "This is David. That's David. Over there is . . . David! So many Davids, only one John," he said. "Hant hant hant."

Now, in his new apartment, I guide guests to him one by one and say, "Here's David."

He falls against them and naps.

If he's not napping, he's shitting.

Every twenty minutes, he jumps up and runs to the john.

"Out of the way," he screams, "out of the way, out of the way!"

I run after him, mopping up the droplets of diarrhea that splatter the floor. He reaches the toilet, and I close the bathroom door behind him and lean against it, facing the crowded room.

* * *

Freud says we place the lost object on a memorial stand, which is not the same as letting it go. We keep it and lose it at the same time. Part of my mind turned into David. David and others. I'm not a man, I'm a crypt filled with dead guys on pedestals in my brain. Dave is my gag writer, long dead. When I say something funny, I'm him.

"How convenient to have a lost object you can plagiarize," Dave says.

* * *

Nathan Lane is in a play. Limited run, sold out. David wants to see it. He'll be dead in three days—literally, not jokingly—so we can't wait for cancellations. He sort of knows the playwright. It's my job to call him. Dave says, "Get him on the phone and tell him I'll just die if I don't see his play."

Dave's off Haldol since his party, which is good news and bad news. The good news is, he's alert again. The bad news is . . .

"Hant hant hant," he'd say.

I track down the playwright's assistant, who has never heard of Dave. "Tell him I'm a semifamous gay author," Dave says. I don't. Nevertheless, the assistant gets us two seats for the next night. Full price, but they're house seats, third row center, and they're Nathan Lane's. Dave is ecstatic. Nathan Lane's house seats. He wants to brag.

Who can he call? No one. He has reached the stage of terminal illness when people figure if you're not dead, you should be. I'm not being harsh. No one wants to say goodbye twice. After all, he had his farewell tour. Threw a party that was really a wake. Why keep staging his exit? People have departure fatigue. Even he does.

So it's just Pepper and me in his living room when Dave says, "I'm going to give Nathan Lane copies of my books! After the play. We will wait at the stage entrance to thank him, and you will hand me each of my books," he tells me, "and I will sign them, and give them to Nathan Lane. And if I hate the play, I won't tell him! I'll just say, 'Nathan Lane, you've done it again!'"

✳ ✳ ✳

We're fifteen minutes late for the curtain when Dave and I show up at the City Center two days before his death. The City Center is a big Moorish revival theater built in 1921 as a meeting place for Shriners— those guys in *Bye Bye Birdie* who watch Janet Leigh do her table dance. If you squint as you head through the gold doors on West Fifty-Fourth Street, you can see twenty-two hundred white men from Warren G. Harding's administration adjusting their red fezzes and filing into the house.

Dave and I have time to picture Shriners because it takes us fifteen minutes to walk from the ticket booth at street level to the lobby one flight down. He's in his uniform of white jeans over diapers, white T-shirt, and blue down coat. Slung on his shoulder is a knapsack that's flat and square and thick and gray as a garment bag doubled in half for hanging shirts and suits on a trunk flight to faraway balls. It holds his portable IV bag. He's getting a pentamidine drip on the run. A clear plastic tube hooked to the IV bag coils out of the knapsack. It slides under his shirt and plugs into the port in his chest.

We walk downstairs while ushers watch. They are figuring out how to seat us. Or how to prevent us from being seated since we're so late and slow. And we're infusing. David is being infused. He's a walking pneumocystis carinii pneumonia prophylaxis. I wonder if anyone has done a pentamidine drip in the house of the Shriners before.

Pentamidine Drip in the House of the Shriners would be a great title for a Tony Kushner play, and I'm about to tell Dave when he says he has to go to the john.

So that solves the problem of getting to our seats. Anyway, for now. One crisis resolved, another in its place. Our life is a drama; who needs plays? We detour to the men's room, where we spend most of Act One.

We're together in the stall. It has a wooden door, which I swing shut, locking us in. He needs me here, not to help him undress, but to hold the pentamidine bag while he shits. He takes his right thumb out of his belt loop, and his pants fall to the floor. Ditto his diapers—he unsticks the Velcro, and they drop.

He squats on the toilet seat. I hear liquid splatter. I don't want to watch, but I don't want to seem like I'm grossed out and turning away. Anyway, in the tiny stall, there aren't many places to look.

"Why are you watching?" Dave says.

"I'm not watching."

"Who would watch this?"

"I said I wasn't watching."

"If I were Liza, and you were Baryshnikov, that would be one thing."

"I'm sorry I'm in the toilet stall with you," I say, which is a sentence you would cut from the film.

"Everybody poops," I almost say. Should I be freaked out by his shit? I'm not saying I'm into it. I can't stand watching needles sink into veins; that's my pitfall as a caregiver. I have penetration anxiety. Blood and shit, though: whatever. Why should either of us be embarrassed? Okay, I wouldn't want anybody in the toilet stall with me, but my body isn't falling apart. Not yet, not from a wasting disease. Will I be grateful that someone who loves me is willing to wipe my ass when I have days to live? "In sickness and health, till death do us part": that's marriage. But David and I are not married—to anyone, nor to each other. My loyalty to him goes beyond what's expected of the unmarried, and that's why I hate marriage. It's smug. There are realms of commitment and intimacy, involving an order of devotion and sacrifice and love, that exceed the terms of anyone's sanctified, legalized marriage.

David is narcissistic, enraged, abusive, accusatory, helpless, wise-cracking, incontinent, and dying. That's what is meant by *dearly beloved*, it turns out.

And this: he sits on the toilet with his pants and diapers on the floor, and I hold his bag high and make sure the plastic tubing has enough give, so it doesn't tear at his chest. His eyes are closed. I wonder if he's falling asleep. When he's done, he asks me for toilet paper. I tear him a length. He wipes and flushes.

Then he wants to check his IV drip. I pull up his T-shirt, and we look at his chest. The port, a white disc. His blue nipples are clipped to his skin. I count his ribs, naming them the way anatomists do. Five are "true," five are "false," and two are "floating" ribs. All twelve are there. We trace the tubing from the port to his knapsack, which I unzip. Dave makes me uncoil, then recoil the tubing. I roll it tight, tuck it away. Re-zip the bag. We get his diapers up, then scoop his pants off the floor and hook his thumb through the belt loop. Then we head back to the ushers, terrifying them.

"Don't hold the curtain," David is shouting, though the play started forty minutes ago. "I mean it. Don't hold the curtain."

The ushers won't seat us. Not even between scenes. Our seats are in the middle of the row, and we'd have to climb over people to reach them. It would be disruptive. Anyway, Act One is about done. The ushers ask us to wait. Dave's yelling, "I'm two minutes from death."

The ushers say okay; we can sit in the aisle, house left. Tiered cement, thinly carpeted. David says okay. We sneak into the back of the house and crouch down on the floor. Dave is sitting on bones.

We're in time for the end of the act. It's a play about AIDS. Naked gay white men with AIDS. We might have stayed in the john. The act ends fast, and now the usher can show us our seats. We get settled, finally. And then Dave has to go to the bathroom again. So we spend

Act Two in the toilet. Same routine: stall, pants, diapers, shit, wipe, port, tube, bag, zip, scream, "Don't hold the curtain for me!"

We miss Act Two. We're in our seats for Act Three, but after ten minutes, Dave falls asleep with his head on my shoulder, where he leaves a circle of drool. He wakes for the curtain call. "It was fabulous," he says. "Wasn't it fabulous?"

We both say it was fabulous. We stand, though standing is hard. The audience applauds, the actors bow, they exit, the stage goes dark, the house lights come up. Audience members file out of the theater until there are just a few people standing near the stage, and Dave and me in our row.

Then Dave turns to me and says, "Now go get Nathan Lane."

I can watch him shit. I can wipe his ass. I can hold the tubing for his pentamidine drip and try to bear the sight of needles piercing his veins. But one thing I cannot do is ask a movie star to talk to me or my dying, or even still living, friend.

"He's not a movie star *yet*," David says. "He's not even really a *Broadway* star! He's an *Off*-Broadway star! I'm a semifamous gay author! So are you! He'll talk to us! We're on the same level of fame!"

Hardly, I say. Don't be bitter, he says. We bicker: Dave expectant, me stalling.

Then, *deus ex machina*, Nathan Lane appears.

Not the Good Witch of the East, not from out of the sky. Not in white or with a wand and the words to hurry us home. But in a burst of light, as velvet curtains part under an Exit sign at the front of the house. Scrubbed free of stage glitter and smiling affably, he comes. Though not summoned. A private audience has not been arranged, not by Dave, not by me.

Divine intervention? He's headed for us. David is yelling his name.

"Nathan Lane, you were fabulous!" he yells. "I'm Dave! A semifamous gay author. I brought you my books!" He points at me. "This is my punk! He's a semifamous gay author, too!"

I'm relieved not to have to wander backstage calling out for Nathan Lane. Then I'm embarrassed, because: um, Dave, who no longer cares what he says or to whom. Then I'm angry at being embarrassed. I don't want to be ashamed of David, not in front of a stranger, certainly not a stranger who's an Off-Broadway star and appears through velvet curtains in a shaft of light.

Now Nathan Lane is standing at our row. A few people still lingering down by the stage move close to hear what he says. Not much. David is running the show. He raises his right hand and says, "Pen!" And I give him a pen. And then he says, "My book!" And I hand him the first of his three published books.

I forgot to say that I've been carrying his books. Go back and add them in: "In my hand, in a bag, in my knapsack hung on my back, I carried David's books." Write a sentence like that, put it where you want. Mention also that it was the last time I saw him alive. He died two days later. Also that I was in shock. And I was protecting everyone else from shock. Which was how I protected myself.

Maybe you don't know, or knew but died, or know but don't want to know how ordinary it was to see emaciated people with pin-straight hair and skin like a sheet thrown over a corpse walking down the street.

By 1994 in New York City, AIDS had become routine, even as it stayed occult, a minority affliction. For a long time it was both unspeakable and widely publicized—staged for your catharsis and relief in New York theaters, a sentimental melodrama that could be managed from the distance of your seats in a packed house.

David wanted to make it extraordinary again. Appalling. Grotesque. To show you how shitty it was. How pierced and diapered and screaming. How relentless and dull. How even death was boring in its incremental ravaging, a day, a day, a day. Boring also in the primal sense of boring into, drilling through flesh into bone, into marrow.

How, when you laughed at David's jokes, you were implicated in the pain from which they arose. Jokes he made in order not to endure his pain but to inflict it.

His theater of cruelty.

I like Nathan Lane too, but that doesn't mean I want to make him watch me die.

Dave talks and talks and signs the books I hand to him. Then he gives them to Nathan Lane. Sometimes I wonder what happened to those books. Are they on a shelf with the Tony Awards? Does Nathan Lane have a story he tells late at night? Did he toss them in the garbage outside the theater? What did I do with my invitation to David's last party? I sent one to myself. Where is the black Mead notebook with Dave's questionnaire? His hospital diary? Did we leave it on Charlotte Sheedy's desk?

After David died, we put his white pants and T-shirts and blue coat and his IV stuff, bags and needles and tubes, in a big red bin for medical waste. Me and Pepper. Then I guess we called a special truck that came and took them away.

* * *

I get proprietary about David. I don't like to hear people talk about him. I don't understand what happened. Sometimes people say, You learn things and move on. Or they say absurd stuff like, God doesn't give you anything you can't handle. God: pfft. And what was there to handle? There was nothing to handle. There was no moving on.

Don't you need to have an experience in order to move on? What experience? What did I learn? David didn't want to die. I was not supposed to let him die. He was dying all the time. Everyone knew he was dying. He knew. He made jokes about it. Saying it to keep it from happening. He *talked* about it constantly, but he would not discuss it. There was no discussion of death. There was no death.

I was forbidden to mention his death, and then he died. It was the most painful thing that ever happened to me. I had nothing left. I had nothing, and then I had nothing left. I wish people would never ask me about him. I wish they would never say his name.

Kid A

You should see the embarrassing poems I've written about him. Andy. Straight guy half my age. Lives with his mom. What was I thinking? After school, when I've been teaching late, I walk from the Queens College campus, two miles through the center of Queens, to the F train in Forest Hills. The F train's a traveling frat house past midnight, dudes slumped low and plugged into earbuds or crowned with headphones. In the early morning, I go home with guys and scribble poems in the backs of books.

It's all I've written for months, these odes to him. To Andy. I scrawled one on the flyleaf of a volume of poetry by Vladimir Mayakovsky. What am I, nineteen? "I Feel My 'I' Is Much Too Small for Me," my poem's called, a quote from Mayakovsy's "Cloud in Trousers."

I wrote another on the last page of Roland Barthes's *The Pleasure of the Text*. Yes, I'm pretentious. And I'm teaching a course in postmodernism. It wasn't my idea. The students asked for it. They heard a rumor I was intertextual, and maybe it's true: I scribble poetry on Barthes.

"Cruising" is the name of the poem in the back of my copy of Barthes. "I'm on a concrete slab in front of Burger King," it starts, and then I want to tell you the time: 2:26 p.m., March 20, the last day before the first of spring, the year 2001. "I'm in East Elmhurst, Queens, New York, Astoria Boulevard, below the flight path of La Guardia Airport."

It's Tuesday afternoon, and the sun is burning off the winter chill. Yo-dudes drive by in SUVs pumping rap. Tractor trailers shift gears, blow smoke. "It's Good for You," a truck advertises. Across the street, which goes both ways, east-west, the Cozy Cabin promises SHOW GIRLS DAILY, its windows masked with cardboard. Uphill from the Cozy Cabin is the Salon del Reino, Kingdom Hall of Jehovah's Witnesses.

God is watching, which is too bad because I've been at the Fair, a porno movie theater. It takes up half a block along Astoria Boulevard at Ninety-First Street. Once a movie palace, now it's a Giuliani-era smut house. Meaning they show kung fu movies in front to hoodwink the vice squad, but in back, past the bathrooms, are three large rooms screening porn. There's a room for hetero sex, a bi room for three-ways, and a room for men-on-men. Girl-on-girl sex is everywhere, except the gay-guy room.

The Fair's porn is polymorphously perverse. Except, again, in the gay-guy room. There won't be two guys kissing onscreen in the hetero room, but the girls will get it on. And straight guys in bi porn get off on watching each other with women. Gay-guy porn, though, is fanatically pure. Anyway, at the Fair. There's no mixing of genders: two guys, or five guys, or ten guys fuck. No pleasure outside of the penis. No pain, either.

I'm gay because I hate, not women, but men. I'm terrified of men, which means that I can't resist them. I want to know how it feels to be a man. I don't want to touch them, I want to be them. Him. Andy's back. If I could press my face to his back, I'm sure I'd be ready for God—for punishment or mercy. I want to be inside him, to know how it feels to swing from that center. Held in by his muscles, pinned and secure. His back, the small of his back. "My ass," he said once, ruefully, meaning, "All my weight's in my ass." It was affectionate and sorry. I want him to talk about me like that. Is that gay? I don't want to be gay. Gay guys are different from men, and I want to be the same as men, which is what *homosexual* means: *resemblance*, not *desire*. I yearn for what I'm not.

I'm not Andy. I'm an untenured assistant professor in a dirty movie theater that runs kung fu films to placate the police. They're shown in the front of the house before a vast empty orchestra and a balcony that is permanently closed. Men linger smoking in the orchestra's foyer, lounging on ratty old couches and chairs. You can sit and chat, or play video games, or stand against the chin-high oak divider behind the last row of auditorium seats, your head in your hands or your arms at your sides, waiting for the fifty-year-old Irish firefighter in work boots and a Mets cap to sidle up to you and let a polite and silent interval pass before he puts his hand on your ass.

East Elmhurst is a middle class Black neighborhood, bordering Corona, which is Mexican and Central and South American, middle class and working class, so the Fair is full of Black guys in sweatsuits and business suits; married Dominican guys—heterosexually married—stepping out; Colombian, Ecuadorian, Peruvian, and Mexican guys who work in restaurants, or public schools, or accounting firms, or law offices, or driving schools, where they teach you how to parallel park. Some of them are probably my students' buddies or bosses. I hope not their dads.

Then there are the married guys—heterosexually married—from Merrick, and Wantagh, and Islip, Long Island, who swing by on their way home, up the Ninety-Second Street exit off the Grand Central Parkway, for a pit stop at the Fair. They're mostly Irish, German, Italian, Greek, Eastern European Jews, carrying attaché cases and glancing repeatedly at their watches.

The age range is forty to sixty. There are a few trans women, but mostly it's cisgender guys, mostly closeted, I'm guessing. A few Asian American kids in their early twenties. East Asian, South Asian, Vietnamese, Chinese, Sri Lankan, Nepali, Filipino, Malaysian.

No one looks like me: doughy WASPy white guy dressed like a preppie in khakis and a Brooks Brothers shirt.

In this place, I'm the Other, which means I'm from Manhattan, I don't have foreskin, I don't speak Spanish, or Russian, or Korean, I don't have children or a wife, I live alone, I'm unbaptized, I don't pray to God. Plus, unlike them, I'm, you know, "gay." Most of the men at the Fair would say they are straight. The story of my life since fifth grade: even in a gay jerk-off parlor, I'm the only fag around.

Everybody plays it straight, in any case. Here's the game:

You hang in the boy-girl porno room for an hour, lounging in the low-slung leatherette reclining seats or standing against the wall, smoking butts and talking with your buddies. Then you wander, just wander, first to the john, then across the hall and quickly as possible through the boy-boy room. You might linger in the bi room for a minute as if you were an anthropologist reading fragments of Icelandic runes. Finally, you turn casually and head to the video buddy booths in back. There are about twenty booths along two short halls. Each booth is the size of a janitor's closet in a New York City middle school.

Today I shared one with my buddy Rico. I think that's what he said his name was, though it might have been "Ricky," or "Rocky," or "Rocco." We didn't have a language in common. I asked his birthday, and he pointed at his watch. "Where do you live?" I said, and again he laid his index finger on the face of his watch. Even if I had been able to speak Spanish, he probably wouldn't have wanted to talk, conversation being, duh, not the point in a stroke parlor. Still, I like to get whatever information I can: name, age, languages spoken, childhood home, astrological sign. I'm not a lonely guy desperate for contact, I'm a census taker. Rico seemed to be close to my age, though he might have been fifty. He was wearing a gold band on his left ring finger. I figured he was a Pisces because he liked to kiss.

If he wasn't my first choice, he also wasn't my last. The whole thing was an accident, really—my being in East Elmhurst at such an hour on such a day. When I left Manhattan this afternoon, I was headed for school. I was due to teach my evening class, where we were going to discuss Barthes' notions of "pleasure" and "bliss." I ended up at a porno movie theater because I got on the wrong train and fell in love with a couple.

They were Russian, and it was the #7 train. I meant to be on the

R. I was buying lunch at Dean & De Luca on Broadway near Houston Street, and there was an N/R train station next door. My face buried in Barthes, I mistakenly got on the N. After crossing under the East River, the train rose above ground, which the R doesn't do. As soon as I saw daylight, I knew I was off track. The N would take me to jail, not college: it ends a bus ride away from Rikers Island. So I switched for the #7 local, which ends at Main Street Flushing, where I could get a bus to campus.

Except that I was hijacked by a guy on the #7 holding his girlfriend's hand. They were speaking Russian, which is odd because Russian immigrants in Queens mostly live along the G or E or F or R, in Forest Hills or LeFrak City. So these two people were out of place. He had a widow's peak, and she was wearing wraparound sunglasses like Yoko Ono. She was small and fine, and he was lanky and wired and stroking her hand. I watched him stroking and stroking her thumb with his hand. He held her fingers laced through his, and he rubbed her thumb with the side of his index finger.

What's the connection that happens between strangers on a train? I'm watching them; they're not aware of me. But they're causing the fuzz at the back of my head and the tight feeling in my stomach. It's like Ernest Hemingway watching a fish. Occupational hazard: as an English teacher, I quote Hemingway, or rather, Nick Adams in "The Big Two-Hearted River," arriving by train at a burned-out town, walking past acres of scorched timber, everything charred and ash—even the grasshoppers' bellies are black—to a bridge across a river. Seeing the water, he thinks, Well, at least the river is there. And in the river are fish, and they are arching out of the water and turning and moving their fins and slicing back into the current. And watching them, in his watching and in their being watched, Nick feels "all the old feeling."

He feels something watching a fish. Of course, the fish doesn't know or care about Nick's feelings. The fish is oblivious to Nick. And just as Nick and maybe Hemingway take pleasure in looking without being noticed or known, so do I. Watching the couple on the train, my head is cottony, and my belly is tight. I'm wondering how it's possible to, whatever, flush red, feel something, have a whole relationship with someone who isn't aware you exist. I'm hooked on people who don't see me. We're tied together, though I'm the only one who senses the taut line from my gut to her finger, his hand. The way he touches and squeezes and caresses her thumb is scary and exciting. It's too much—he won't leave her alone; he leans over her and grabs her free hand, and doesn't let go. If I were her, I'd ask him to stop. But I don't want him to stop.

When they get off the train at Elmhurst Avenue and Ninetieth Street, six stations ahead of mine, I'm pulled out after them by the strength of the connection they don't see or suspect. My following them feels involuntary, which is not to say I don't know it's invasive: I'm a grown man on my way to teach a roomful of graduate students about "jouissance," and I have turned, halfway there, into a stalker, a Hemingway quoter, a creep.

Out on the train platform, she goes on ahead, and for a minute, I think they've separated because he's suddenly alone. His hair is sandy brown and thinning in front, and I don't think he buys his own clothes. The sheer shirt and the pants—white painter's pants tight at the waist—seem like her choice. He's got a brown mole on his right cheek, thick blunt fingers, wide shoulders, and a funny walk. He nearly skips after her when he finds her down on the street. There she is, ahead of him, and he races to reach her, putting his arms around her shoulders and neck from the back.

I know I'm being invasive. I want to call the police on myself. So I lose them, walking to Ninety-Second Street and turning north, heading up through Jackson Heights to East Elmhurst, "accidentally" reaching the Fair.

You never "decide" to go into a porno house. Anyway, I don't. It's not like planning a trip to the mall. Suddenly, I'm here. "Oh, look, gay porn, who knew?" Except I walked here directly, if leisurely, all the while telling myself that it's a pleasant day to stroll through the neighborhoods of Queens. Forget that I've got class to teach in two hours. Until the last half-block, when I make a deliberate turn into the entryway of the movie theater, I'm convinced I have other plans. I'll stop at a payphone, call Andy, pray his mom doesn't answer. "Yo, dude. I'm in East Elmhurst, which, to get here from Elmhurst, you have to walk *north*. Figure that." Then I'll snag a cab on Astoria Boulevard and reach school way before class.

Except, there are never any cabs in East Elmhurst. And the route to Queens College, by way of surface roads, is blocked at almost every turn by huge highways. You see my problem. Why not go jerk off? I pass through the theater's gaping entryway, under the giant marquee— First Run In Queens, it says, coyly, as if you could walk inside and catch the latest Hollywood action blockbuster—pay my dough to the Guyanese Indian American guy behind the ticket booth, spin through the turnstile, and enter the Fair.

Like all the guys, I start in the boy-girl room. But I can't watch porn for long. It wouldn't matter if Aamir Khan were doing Tony Leung, or Gong Li were smooching Halle Berry. Porno makes everything look like a training film for garage mechanics: in, out, shaft, piston.

Is that all there is?

After a minute, I cross the hall, through the boy-boy room, past the bi room, to the buddy booths. Lining the halls are maybe twenty guys, potential buddies, their faces creased as sharecroppers in a photo-essay by Walker Evans. Men with big hands and chipped nails, men with their hair combed carefully in place, men in blue jeans and parkas, plain men. I think of immigrants to New York in the early 1900s, when guys on their own in lower Manhattan got tired of putting off sex until the day they had money enough to send home for their girlfriends and wives. So they went to a huge beer house on the

Bowery, where boys gowned like Gibson girls served drinks and then had sex for pay in rooms upstairs.

That makes public sex between men sound quaint and historic. But I'd be lying if I didn't admit that the Fair is depressing. With men, there's always a game, and the winner of every porno palace is the guy who gets to reject the most people. The victor today is an Italian American guy who looks like Robert De Niro in *The Godfather II*. De Niro's stand-in. He's strutting, angular, groomed, compact, well-dressed, quick-moving, all business. If you glance at him, he frowns. Lighting cigarettes, checking his watch, he has convinced himself that he's at a board meeting closing a deal or scouting leftie pitchers. Anything but prowling the oiled halls of a crumbling smut house for a guy who'll put a finger up his butt.

Here is how I know I'm not a man: men are people who can stand completely grim and immobile for hours dreaming of sex. In strip parlors, they lounge at the lip of the stage, not moving, while someone gorgeous squats naked above them, legs spread. Slumped in chairs in porno theaters, they sit inert as rutabaga bulbs watching naked people flash exquisite body parts across the screen. In the hallways of the Fair, guys stand still as if mounted on corkboard, maybe not even alive. Pornographic sex is obviously a sedative. It doesn't excite; it deflates. The problem with American youth is that they don't watch *enough* pornography. Mothers, if you want your children docile and depressed, send them to the smut house.

In other words, I'm walking around and no one is checking me out. Half an hour's gone. I'm running out of time. I paid $8.50 at the door, I want my money's worth of joy. Which is when Rico turns up. I'm circling the halls for the seventeenth time, and he's in the corner, next to the fire door, and he looks at me. No smile, nothing that nice. Just a glance, our eyes meet, and that's my signal. Is he attractive? Sure, everyone's attractive. Especially when you're running out of time. I'm a fatalist with sex: if you happen to want me, I'm yours. Which sometimes gets me in trouble. Though not here, if *trouble* means falling in love. You don't fall in love in video booths, except for ten minutes, and I've got twenty. Rico steps into a booth, and I follow.

He shuts the door. There's a tiny TV screen near the door showing four channels of porn: guy-in-leather; guy-in-gym-shorts; girl-with-tongue-stud. The other channel is static. Sometimes men who go with you into a booth will watch the screen, not you, while you both jerk off. Rico puts his arms around me, hugs me, kisses my neck. I'm leaning against the wall. A knee-high bench is built into the wall, and I take off my coat and put it on the bench with my knapsack.

Inside my knapsack is a $7.00 tuna fish sandwich that I bought at Dean & DeLuca, thinking, I'll save this for later. I didn't want to eat on the train because I was lost in *The Pleasure of the Text*. Barthes kept talking about "hermeneutics," which is Greek for "interpretation," though it also kind of means "money": it's from a root word for "assigning values to things you exchange." Rico has got his hand in my pants. He is rubbing my penis through my boxer shorts, which I bought at the K-Mart on Astor Place after Andy told me that he got all his underwear at "the pharmacy."

"What pharmacy?'" I said.

"Any pharmacy," he told me.

Then Andy lifted his shirt and showed me his shorts, which, like all men in America under the age of thirty, he wears way above the waist of his jeans. There was the sudden aching gap of skin between his shirt and shorts. "Is not the most erotic portion of the body *where the garment gapes*?" Barthes asks in *The Pleasure of the Text*, his words jutting into italics. Whenever you see "skin flashing between two articles of clothing," he says, "it is this flash itself which seduces." And quickly disappears, which is the true joy: knowing joy will end. In other words, bliss is loss. Desire is whatever you're losing.

"You'll lose money buying them anywhere else," Andy said, and he was right. K-Mart was selling three pairs of boxer shorts for $9.95, way cheaper than the Gap. I bought nine pairs. The pair that Rico is rubbing his flat palm against is white with red pencil stripes.

Then he undoes my zipper.

Suddenly there's a dead guy in the room with me. Not Rico, but David. Always the dead best friend, tagging along. I'm Norman Mailer: mention sex, I'm instantly thinking of death. Or I'm a gay man who has lived in New York for twenty-one years—for these *particular* twenty-one years—and everything and reminds me of death. Dave died eighteen months before all the new life-saving drugs became available. Up until the last few months of his life, he was delightfully silly. Mention sex to Dave, and he came up with not death but a party game:

"In the movie of your life, who would play your penis?" Dave asks from the grave—which, considering that I've got Rico's hand in my pants, is kind of wrecking the moment. Placating David's ghost, I say, "Angela Bassett."

"That's cheating," he says.

"All right. Eric Stoltz."

"Eric *Stoltz*?"

"You know, sturdy, pink, supportive. Not the lead but often an intriguing cameo. Better for television, really: small-screen, German Irish, completely functional, thank you very much, and secretly capable of wacky outbursts. Stoltz means 'pride' in German," I add, modestly.

That silences David. He's gone. The dead want to name my dick, but Rico, the living, is holding it, pulling it out of my pants. Now I'm a fully dressed man in a booth talking silently with a ghost while a stranger in jeans and a T-shirt gets my penis out in the open, poking naked through my shorts and zipper.

He's touching it. Which completely banishes David, thank God. I'm alive, and I won't lie: there's the wonderful encompassing shock of a guy putting his hand all the way around your penis.

"What's your name?" I ask him, because if you touch my penis, I'm in love with you, and I want to hear him speak, this object of my love. I ask again, "What's your name?" He's just my height; his hair is fine and brown. He leans back and pulls off his shirt, and there's a cross on a chain hanging on his chest, and I'm thinking, "Jesus hung out with tax collectors, who is He to judge?"

There isn't much hair on his chest. His belly is big but solid. He undoes my pants and pulls my trousers and shorts to my knees, and then he raises my T-shirt and shirt and sweater—I'm wearing a powder blue sweater vest, which makes me look Republican—and kisses my nipple, the left one, over my heart.

Well, he's holding me. My trousers and shorts are at my ankles. "What," I ask him, closing my eyes, putting my arms around his back, wondering if I should take off my watch, which is big and blocky with the face on the inside, against my inner wrist. I'm scraping my watch across his back as I stroke his shoulders. But if I take it off, I'll forget it. So I harrow his back. His head is under my T-shirt and shirt and sweater vest. "What," I repeat, "is your name?"

Our video screen is tuned to boy-in-leather, who's saying, "Faggot, suck my dick."

I never understand the preferred conceit of gay male porn, which is that somebody has to not want it. There's one guy who's straight and won't do it, and a faggot who constantly does. Though I guess that's me and everyone I've ever loved. On the other hand, Rico kisses me. He comes out from under my shirt and T-shirt and kisses me on the lips. He kisses me quick, once, twice, wraps himself entirely around me, holds me as tight as he can, kisses me again. We're kissing for real, now, and I'm thinking, Well, I hope he doesn't have herpes. Then I remember that there are other things I don't yet know about him: his name and whether he has a functioning penis.

I undo his fly, unsnap his trousers, unbuckle his belt, and push down his pants. He's wearing pink bikini underwear, which means for certain that he doesn't speak English. He pulls his underwear down, and I say again, holding his penis—I take it in my hand not greedily or expectantly, or as if it were ever my right, but with an air of what Tennessee Williams would call "tender protection"—I guess I *am* a fag; I can't touch a strange man's penis without quoting Tennessee Williams. I ask him again, "What's your name?" And that's when he tells me, with his dick in my hand. "Rico," he says, or "Ricky," or, "Rocco," or, "Rocky," or "Enrique," or maybe he misunderstood, maybe he was answering another question that I didn't think I'd asked.

So now we're two guys naked to the ankles. Or, rather, he's naked; I'm not. So I get shirtless too. I think sides are supposed to be even. I drop my shirts and sweater to the bench with my knapsack and coat, and we're both nude with our pants and shorts around our feet. He's sucking my nipples again.

"That's right, faggot," says the guy on the video, which is, like, flashback to high school. I hit the channel button and change it to static.

Rico and I kiss for a long time. Our skin pressed together, shoulder to thigh, we kiss. He won't talk, but he likes to kiss. My watch has a button that lets you light its face to see the time, and I press it: still an hour before school. I lean back. He's jerking me off. I hold his penis. He has lumpy testicles held up close to his groin, and his penis is shaped like him, blunt and big-headed, but, unlike him, oddly aloof.

He's sucking my nipples like I have taken my only son in my arms and nursed him, my hand on the back of his head, saying, "Rico," over and over, "Rico," softly, and he doesn't make a sound. His penis is Christopher Walken. It's part of the action, but it doesn't belong in this film or any film. Maybe a French film, not this sloppy human American thing in which a grown man suckles another full-grown man with pink bikini underwear tangling in his shoelaces. And suddenly Rico yells, or, really, cries, and he comes on my thighs, and all over my discount K-Mart boxer shorts that Andy got me to buy.

He comes and I don't. I smile apologetically. It's an unwritten smut-house rule that you both come at once, so your buddy doesn't have to get you off when he's already splattered. But Rico smiles wistfully, and then, kindly and patiently, he holds me with his arm around my shoulders, and his head pressed to my neck while he jerks me off. He's watching, we're both watching me. Because in the second before I come—more smut-house etiquette—I have to turn sharply away so that I blast, not on us, or on the bench where my bag is packed with lunch and Roland Barthes, but against the wall and on the floor, so no one gets slimed or soaked.

I'm done. We don't speak. He dresses quickly, but he waits while I clean up, which takes a while because my shorts are shot. They're wet with him. I have to remove my shoes, my trousers, and shorts, wad Andy's boxers, wipe myself with them, and drop them on the bench, leaving them behind.

He watches and waits. When I'm dressed, he grins, hugs me, turns to go, reaches out, his palm and fingers outstretched—"Every narrative," Barthes says, "is a staging of the absent father"—and touches my face. "Later, man," I tell him. He goes out the door, I close it, wait a second, lean against the wall, close my eyes, remember, remember his hand.

Because joy, for me, isn't just sex. Sure, I liked him touching my dick. But it would have been okay if he'd wanted something else, if he'd asked to be dandled or paddled or tweaked. There was a guy once who called me his "queer buddy" and told me to tie his work boots to his testicles. "Whatever, man," I said. I don't mind what anyone wants. The payoff, for me, the value-exchange, is in the moment afterward, when we're dressed again as men, and he doesn't speak English, and I don't speak anything else, and he hugs me, and it's like, "Yo, man, I'm so alone."

There's my joy: how men are lonely.

I'm in love with male loneliness.

Women are supposed to be lonely. Doomed to loneliness, without men. I learned that from Bette Davis. Her power, her self-sufficiency, had made her lonely, on film and in life. "Nothing's any good unless you can look up just before dinner, or turn around in bed, and there he is," she says, in *All About Eve*. I grew up thinking I would be a lonely woman who missed men. I didn't learn until later how lonely *men* are. Lonely for other men. Lonely because they're forced to *be* men.

Can I have that moment with you? Can I have that masculine distance, disappearance, vanishing, remove, aloofness, withdrawal, that silent moment after sex with someone whose name I don't know who sucked my nipples, held my penis, cried like a child, and spilled himself across my thighs? He was helpless in that instant. The best thing about sex is helplessness, the stuff you can't do. He couldn't not come. And afterward, he put his hand on my face and said, "'Bye." In whatever language. And I said, "Goodbye."

Outside, I check my watch, which, thankfully, I didn't leave in the porno booth. I've got time before I head to school, so I sit in front of Burger King on Astoria Boulevard and eat my sandwich from Dean & DeLuca.

When I'm done, I walk along Astoria Boulevard to the Van Wyck Expressway, taking the beautiful curve of the entrance ramp up into traffic. I'm a grown man walking along an expressway. It's spring: cars honk, not happily; people think I'm a jerk. Getting off the highway, I climb over concrete dividers, cut through traffic on entrance and exit ramps, reach grass, come to the big empty parking lot of Shea Stadium, which is blue. Then I'm on Roosevelt Avenue, on a bridge that goes over the Van Wyck Expressway and under the Flushing #7 train. This is where Nick Carraway and Tom Buchanan got off the train to visit Tom's lover Myrtle in Fitzgerald's valley of ashes. It's now a junkyard for wrecked cars, and it smells of sewage and vegetable rot.

Spin around and you can get a whiff of industrial waste and a panoramic view of, you know, the postmodern condition. Texts competing for attention, equally insistent. Identity built from contradictory fragments that lead away from your "self" into nothing. I become what I see: the bruise-red cars of the Flushing local sinking underground across rusted switches and tracks. Planet Earth the graying 1964 World's Fair Unisphere. All the parkways and expressways, bloodlines Robert Moses laid through the bog, curl around each other like live bait in a soup can. And a sign across the Flushing River says SELF STORAGE.

And if I could have talked to Rico, I would have said, with guy-like sentimentality, not embarrassed, "Man, I love New York." Wreckage and disaster. I love looking at this intersection of highways and trains and planes taking off overhead and cars crashed and the river stagnant below and thinking, This is all we can do, this is the best we can ever do; we get off the boat from faraway places and build across the new land a redeemer nation of what? Sewage, slop, waste, rot, rusted steel, the gaping awful failure of a century. Face-to-face with man's capacity for wonder, and we make ourselves, in Flushing, a mess.

Not Manhattan's mess. Manhattan is the pores of the face scrubbed clean. The rest of the body is here, God's blood and guts and soul and wounds and all. I love the failing body, knowing we'll die. I love the clogged river and the airplanes and the Mets, the fucking Mets. Because the other thing I want is to be nothing. Queens is a good place for that. There are lonely men everywhere here waiting to leave you so they can get close at the last minute. That's bliss. That's when I feel joy, when I want to be "present." Well, here I am: leaving you, drifting past, hand on your face, reeking of come, headed for nothing, happy with that. It won't take a moment. Andy. Just give me your hand.

It Must Be Swell to Be Laying Out Dead

David is shaking uncontrollably when I walk into his hospital room, Tuesday morning, ten days from his death. He's tucked in tight, wrapped in a shroud, his white sheet pulled to his chin and his body shaking so hard that the sheet ripples down to his toes.

I have never seen anybody shake like that.

It's a special effect in a science fiction film.

He weighs ninety pounds, down from one-hundred-fifty one month ago.

How can I help him? I'm not a doctor. He's my best friend, but he doesn't want me to touch him. He doesn't like to be touched. Not by me, not now.

So what are my options?

I can climb into his bed and hold him until he stops shaking.

I can get him some blankets.

I can run for a nurse.

I can fall to my knees and cry to God or Buddha or whomever.

Bad choices. He doesn't want help to die. He doesn't want to die.

I leave his room and run to the nurses' desk. A nurse is sitting there looking at me, and I don't know how to ask her for help because I can't think of what to call Dave. His relationship to me. He's sort of my husband. Can I say that? "My husband is shaking really bad?" Gay men don't have husbands. Not yet. Not for a while. "Husband," though. It has authority, makes a recognizable claim. It would get them to listen. His health would matter if Dave and I were married or related, or . . . "My brother? Needs your help?" Anyone can see we're not brothers. What matters to them, other than marriage or blood? "My closest friend?" That's a lie, in any case. Dave doesn't let anyone get close to him, not even me—especially not me. "My lover?" You have to be Eartha Kitt or European to get away with "my lover." And he's not. We have never been lovers.

He's the first person I speak to each day, the last one at night. Phone calls early and late. Every day for the past five years has started and ended with Dave.

He's the center of my life, that's all.

"The center of my life in the room down the hall needs help?"

Language isn't much good.

So I settle on: "David? The guy over there? Is kind of shaking really hard? And I wonder if someone has noticed or talked to the doctor or something?"

Why am I not Shirley MacLaine in *Terms of Endearment*, circling the room and shouting for drugs?

"He's shaking really hard," I say. "It's scary."

The nurse looks up. "Oh, yeah," she says. "We'll send someone in a minute."

"In, in a minute?"

She nods.

In a minute, he'll fly apart like a spaceship hitting the atmosphere without a heat shield.

"A minute," I say, and she nods again, and I go back to his room because death is all plot, and you have to watch it. Okay, you can choose not to. Those are your only options: watch it or flee. But it happens, that's all it does. It happens, and happens, and happens.

"Sit and talk to me," Dave says, still shaking.

"Are you cold?"

"Don't ask questions."

"All right."

"All right, what?"

"All right, I'm touching your forehead," I say, which he can't prevent. He's shaking too hard to resist, and his forehead is warm.

"I'll be right back," I tell him, and I go to the nurses' station again.

"Look," I say, "I don't mean to be an asshole, I'm sure you have a difficult job, but he's really shaking, and he looks cold, but his head's warm, and I wonder if maybe you could deal with it now."

"I know," the nurse says. "We called the resident. He'll be here in a minute."

"Maybe a minute's too long," I say. "It's just that it seems really bad."

"I know."

So she knows. I go back to his room, and this time someone follows me with a blanket. David says he's cold, but the cold is coming from the inside out, and the blanket is cosmetic. The nurse tucks it under his chin, and I think, Great, now he looks like somebody shaking really hard in a blanket.

"Does your doctor know about this?" I ask him.

"John," he warns. He hates when I help, and he screams when I don't.

"Why don't I call your doctor?" I say.

"Okay, call him."

"All right, I'm sorry, but here's another question. I'm sorry. I can't believe I don't know this. What's his number?"

"Jesus," he says. "No, no, no, I'll get it. I wrote it down in my book."

He won't let me look for his phone book. He wants to find it himself. I know where it is. When I go to help him, he yells.

"Don't touch anything."

It's in the top drawer of his bedside table, in front, on the left.

"Here it is," he says, holding it out to me in his trembling hand. "Here here here."

Naturally, I can't find his doctor's number.

"Do you have the number?" he says.

"Yes," I lie. For a second, I think I am going to have to dial information while he watches and waits. That would be the worst thing. His watching, his waiting for me to do something he expects me not to be able to do. Then I see the doctor's number in the margin of a page.

"Here it is," I say, and David says, "Dial nine first. You have to dial nine to get an outside number."

Why is this what bugs me? His telling me how to use the phone?

"David," I say. "I've used this phone before. I know how to use this phone."

"You dialed 9?"

"I'm dialing it now."

"Maybe it's the antibiotics."

"Maybe what's the antibiotics?"

"I'M TAKING NEW ANTIBIOTICS," he yells. "Jesus Christ."

"So you're having a drug reaction."

"It *might* be a drug reaction."

He's still yelling. I'm dialing the phone, it's ringing, someone answers. A voice I don't know. Not the doctor.

"I'm calling for a patient," I say, and I tell the voice my name, and I say Dave's name, clearly and plainly, like giving directions to cab drivers. I don't want to have to repeat anything with David watching me. His eyes behind his thick glasses are floodlights.

"Hi, Don," the phone voice says.

"*John*," I say, amazed that I care right now if anybody gets my name right.

"What's he saying?" David asks.

"It's not the doctor," I say, covering the mouthpiece.

"This is not the doctor," the voice says.

"Did you tell him I'm shaking?"

"I'm not talking to the doctor."

"Tell him I'm shaking."

"It's the receptionist or someone."

"I don't care if it's the fucking receptionist," David yells, and I uncover the mouthpiece in time for the phone voice to hear that.

"David is shaking," I say.

"Shivering," he yells.

"Shivering uncontrollably."

"My teeth are chattering."

"His teeth are chattering."

"Let me give you the doctor, all right?" the receptionist says.

"What is he doing?" Dave says.

"Getting the doctor."

"That wasn't the doctor?"

"I said it wasn't the doctor."

"What?"

"I said it's not the doctor, but they're getting the doctor."

"Tell him I'm shivering and my teeth are chattering."

"That's what I'm going to do."

"What?"

"I said, Dave, that's what I'll do."

Then the doctor is on the phone.

I repeat everything, my name, Dave's name, "I'm at St. Vincent's—"

"He knows that, John."

"Right," the doctor says.

"And he's shaking uncontrollably."

"Shivering," David says.

"Shivering uncontrollably."

"And what else?" the doctor says.

"And my teeth are chattering," Dave yells. "CHATTERING."

"Maybe from the new drugs," I say.

"NOT YET," David screams. "I'M NOT TAKING THE NEW DRUGS YET. JESUS FUCKING CHRIST."

"Okay, okay, okay," I say, covering the mouthpiece. "How am I supposed to know that?"

"I don't have him on anything new at the moment," the doctor says. "We'll see what happens when he gets home. He's going home tomorrow."

"Yes," I say, "I'm surprised about that, aren't there more tests—"

"I DON'T NEED ANY MORE FUCKING TESTS."

"All right, Dave," I say. I lower the phone. "All right." I put the phone back to my ear. "Anyway," I say. "He's still shaking."

"Have you talked to the nurses?"

"Yes."

"Fine."

"They said they would send somebody."

"That's fine."

"Are you coming?"

"I'll be in later this afternoon. It might be his catheter."

"His catheter?"

"They changed the tubes hooked to my catheter," David says, no longer shouting, sounding resigned, "early this morning. That's when I got chills."

"I'll check him later," the doctor says.

"Is it my catheter?"

"All right then?"

"Is it?"

The doctor hangs up.

"I don't know, David," I say. "He didn't tell me. He's gone."

Then the resident arrives with nurses. Dave yells, "Fuck you, fuck you, be careful," and they make him sit up and lift his hospital shift, and they press metal to his chest and listen. They push him forward and listen to his back. I can see all the ribs in his back. The doctors ask him to breathe. He breathes. There is no flesh to press the stethoscope against; they are listening to bone. They take blood. I watch the needle go in, hoping it doesn't make me sick.

They take his blood pressure, they feel around his belly, they check the tubes attached to the needle in his arm and the catheter in his chest. They jiggle the bags hanging from the rolling metal tree that holds the plastic sacks of liquid draining into him, some of the liquid passing first in clear tubes through a big metal box with dials that light up and a keypad like on an ATM.

Then the resident and the nurses and aides go away, and I'm alone with David again.

He lies back and closes his eyes, and I pull a chair close to his bed and sit, resting my arms on the mattress.

I watch him. He's still shaking. I still can't figure out how to help him. He shakes for an hour, he shakes less and less, he falls asleep—it seems like he's asleep; his eyes are closed, but his lips are moving. I lean forward to hear what he's saying. He stops shaking, but his lips are moving. If he's whispering something, I can't tell what it is. I sit for hours, bent over him, trying to hear, as close as I can get without touching.

Katherine Mansfield

A subway! In Hollywood. How likely was that? I caught it at Hollywood and Vine. It was at the bottom of an escalator. The stacked platters of the Capitol Records Building disappeared, disc by disc, as I sank down to a tunnel that had been carved through shifting tectonic plates and geological faults. Who knew LA had a basement? I felt oddly safe under the desert. How could there be pain in such an imaginary realm? Yet there was more reality underground than up above: no palm trees, no implausibly temperate weather, but rather train tracks, people on the platform reading tabloids, a long wait, and then the train as heavy as a cluster headache riding into the station.

I was in town to see Marc, whose life I ruined twice in ten years. There was a chance I'd do it again. I guess that's why he flew me out to see his latest work in progress. He needed more heartbreak. For inspiration? For good luck? He had written a musical. Though he was an indie rock star, he was secretly in love with Rodgers and Hammerstein, and he had taken a commission to write an emo musical called *I'm Sick of You*. It was premiering at the Disney Center in downtown LA, and he said it was a cross between *The Sound of Music* and *Death in Venice*. "It's about a nun and an overripe strawberry," he told me, "and you." Not me! I'm a terrible muse. I disappear on contact and run away when you call. Except sometimes I don't.

We hadn't spoken in months when Marc phoned one night to summon me to Los Angeles.

He said, "I'm on the roof of my hotel."

It was four in the morning on the Lower East Side. He had forgotten the time difference. Or not. I decided to be harsh. "Are you planning to jump?"

"No comment," Marc said.

He had a voice so deep it was like talking to Lurch. On his records, he sped up his vocal tracks, which raised his voice a tone, but he was famous for sounding like an open crypt. It was part of his goth charm. Still, he could be sweet. If he sang high, his voice cracked like Frank Sinatra regretting Ava Gardner in "I'm a Fool to Want You." He thought of himself as a bummed teen, making basement miasma music with his medicated pals, but he was thirty-eight, a Brill Building tunesmith with a Bowery loft and a Geffen contract. *Less Is Less* was the name of his hit CD, recorded with his band Katherine Mansfield. It won the *Village Voice* Pazz and Jop Poll, where Robert Christgau called it "Burt Bacharach with a migraine," which he meant as praise. Marc kept threatening to hire session musicians and put out an airtight polished disc as if he were Phil Spector without the girl problem and the handgun, but he liked a basement sound and the odd instruments that he picked up at yard sales, and despite his Starbucks airplay, he would never be slick.

"You're not going to die by leaping from a roof," I said. "You're a rock star, you'll be shot by a fan. Or found floating face-down in a swimming pool."

"Or in a double overdose with the one I love," he said, hopeful.

"Or you'll gag on a tuna fish sandwich."

"And choke on my own puke." He was laughing, which was not a good sign. Marc's laughter celebrated the death of love. He had never loved anyone in his whole life—including himself—except me. I don't like myself so much that I want two of me around. But that's what it was like to be with Marc. He abandoned himself and escaped as quickly as possible into you. He was willing to pay rent on the shared space. I'm not saying he was ungenerous. He was extremely generous, in thanks for not much. I'd like to say that I ran like hell as soon as I got free—not once, but twice—but the fact is, I still owe him twelve hundred bucks.

"I had a dream that I was in your bedroom last night," he said, "and you were fast asleep, but there was a light still lit above your bed, and I tried to turn it off, but it wouldn't go out."

"Is this a song?'

"There were plenty of switches. I tried them all. I unscrewed the bulb."

"You're calling me up because you need to write a song, and I'm the only guy who makes you feel bad enough to do it."

"Even when I screwed the bulb loose, you were still lit."

"That was a dream. I don't glow."

"It's not going well," he said, finally. "The musical. Our showcase opens in a week, and my songs still don't have any 'buttons.' I'm making shirts, apparently. And the second song of every musical is supposed to be an 'I want' song. I said I don't do 'want.' I only do 'didn't get.' They put *My Fair Lady* on my iPod. I'm meant to listen to it every night. I said I'd rather eat lightbulbs than listen to *My Fair Lady*." He started singing. "All I want is a fifty-watt lightbulb I can chew, and you, and you, and you." He stopped. "Will you come out here?" he said. "And stay with me?"

There was a long pause.

"If you were here," he said, "we *could* jump, forty stories, and we'd splatter on the asphalt, under a streetlight. Please come? I'll pay the flight. You can stay in my room. I'm in a big new downtown hotel. The bathtub's the size of an apartment on Avenue A."

"Am I supposed to show up and then flee every time you need a new song?"

"You didn't 'flee,' you dumped me. Twice."

"I took you to breakfast. Anyway, the first time."

"You took me to Elephant and Castle and dumped me over brioche."

"And you went straight home and wrote ten exquisite little acid rock songs about it. Did you write them in your own blood?"

"No comment."

"And you won every music poll in the country. Your songs are playing all over Lower Manhattan. Still. I turned on the TV last night, you're the background for a rental-car commercial. You sold our breakup to Hertz."

"National."

"Third-string rental cars, thanks."

"I'll fly you here first-class. How can you leave me again if we're three thousand miles apart?"

"There's your 'I want' song. You've written it already."

He sighed heavily—a worrisome sigh, because he meant it. Normally Marc was careful not to mean anything. He was all about style emptied of specific content. We were so used to talking to each other in sterling epithets that it took an audible gasp to switch from arch to earnest. Now I was in trouble. He was about to be sincere. Sincerity is my Kryptonite. It strips off my fabulous cape and leaves me feeling stunned and human. Too bad I can't resist it. In spite of myself, I crave the literal-minded. All my life, I have wanted to marry someone prosaic, and the people I have yearned for most have been the ones who don't really get me. They never know when I'm kidding, and so they keep their distance. Ironists like Marc, on the other hand, are drawn to me like woodchucks to the false spring, and I have been loved continuously since high school by failed poets and lapsed Catholics and bitter guys from Boston who died cursing God but were buried nonetheless clutching their rosary beads.

Unlike my dead friends, Marc's self-lacerating turned a profit. It gave him energy and power and tapped into his talent and fed his increasing renown. He was rewarded everywhere for his brilliance, while I had a hard time getting tenure at a service college in Flushing.

Was I jealous? I will say that when Marc called from California to tell me things were not going well, I was kind of thrilled.

We were both quiet a minute. "I'm serious," he said. He was whispering now. "I have no idea if my stuff is good. Which has never happened before. Even worse, everyone treats me like I'm perfect. But if I were perfect, you'd want me."

"I never said you weren't perfect."

"I need someone here who's not a fan. And I trust your judgment. It's warm here," he added. "I'm wearing a T-shirt."

He knew I hated March in New York.

"I can't spare more than the weekend," I said. "And I won't stay with you."

"Forget I suggested it."

"There's a cheap motel on Hollywood Boulevard, if that's not redundant," I said. Years ago, I had moved to LA, where I stuck it out for a summer. When I got back to New York, I hinted that some tragedy had forced me to leave California, but the fact was, nobody had discovered me in a drugstore on Sunset Boulevard, and I came home. "It can't be more than sixty bucks a night," I said, "even now."

"Then you'll come?"

Yes. I said I would come. Because why? Because he must have known abrupt departure excites me. Because I wanted to be wearing a T-shirt and driving with the top down up La Cienega Boulevard at midnight. In LA, you could be alone in the middle of things. The city was not built high, it was spread flat, with people scattered across it like pieces flung from a clenched fist onto a game board. You were never more than fifteen minutes away from being alone on a blue hill surrounded by scrub oak and looking down at everything.

Because—I don't really understand friendship. If you're in extreme need, I'm your best friend. Otherwise, I'm not there. There's no second act in my life, but there's a first and a third. I don't do middles. I'll stick around to fall in love and watch you die, but nothing in between.

I'm good in a crisis.

But what if the disaster you needed to be rescued from was me? What were my responsibilities then?

Was I a vaccine you shot in your arm until you grew resistant to my charm?

That was one of Marc's songs about me. It was on my iPod, and I sang along as the Red Line train pulled into my station and took me downtown to see my two-times ex.

✳ ✳ ✳

Marc says the subject of all pop songs is other pop songs—it's in an interview in *Rolling Stone*—and I guess he's right because he was already writing our breakup song two weeks after we met. That was eight years ago, the first time we were boyfriends. We lasted mere months, June to September. Ten days after our first date, I went out of town for the weekend, and when I got back, Marc had his song. It was called "Painless," a pun—Payne is my middle name. My parents' mean joke. Marc stuck it in a tune he had started years ago and stashed in a drawer because it was lacking something: me. It had been waiting for me to show up and then run off. Not even run, because I wasn't missing yet. I had been away for thirty-seven hours. Marc needed to lose me, and I felt posthumous around him, always already gone. "Painless" is the first cut on *Less Is Less*, which came out five years after we broke up. All its songs end in *less*, and they are all about me, or missing me: "Heartless," "Ruthless," "Loveless," etc. Maybe the point of pop music is to remind you of pop music, but what if you're Warren Beatty, and the song really *is* about you?

Our first boyfriendhood started in the cobblestone yard of St. Mark's Church in the Bowery. Manhattan was having its truncated spring, and Marc was out regretting it as it passed. He was with one of his bearded, bearish, elaborately punctilious friends, who, like a docent at the Metropolitan Museum of Art, was delivering a brief lecture on *Aspiration* and *Inspiration,* the two stone statues of Indigenous Americans with ripped abs and giant hands that flank the entrance to the church. They were sculpted by Solon Borglum, a Danish Mormon from Utah whose brother had designed Mount Rushmore. These facts were imparted by the bearded friend, who had flagged me down when he saw me walking up Second Avenue. I knew him, but I couldn't remember his name.

I had last seen him, Marc's bearded buddy, at a memorial service. He belonged to a period in my life that had only just ended when all my friendships were conducted in sickrooms and funeral parlors. My best friend had died the previous fall. Marc had just moved to the East Village from Philadelphia, where he had lived for ten years, and where he had left behind his boyfriend-since-college. We were both recently split off from a hunk of our past, and we clung to each other almost from the moment we met, in the June breeze that would not be sweet with the promise of new life for more than another few days.

It was a summer romance. We were broke, living in tiny, hot, airless East Village apartments, though he had just released two CDs on independent labels, and he was being courted by executives from big record companies. He was epically rude to all of them. I never knew anyone so hostile to success who was nonetheless doomed to have it. No doubt his contemptuous tone was taken as a sign of his genius. Rock stars are supposed to be sociopaths. He insisted all summer that what he wanted wasn't a major label record deal, but me. But when we started dating, we had both hoped it wouldn't last. He was looking for someone new to lament, and I was still transfixed by a corpse—my dead best friend.

"What was he like?" Marc asked, one night, a few weeks after we met. We were in bed in my apartment. It was August, in the worst of the humidity. Hip young couples were having first dates in the refrigerated meats section of the Key Food on Avenue A. Marc bought a tiny portable air conditioner, and we set it up in my bedroom and stripped down and took turns exposing various of our body parts to the blasts of cool air.

We were having the conversation where new lovers list their exes. I was playing it like the scene from Godard's *Breathless*: Jean Seberg and Jean-Paul Belmondo jump around a tiny Paris apartment, from bed to bathroom and back to bed. Belmondo asks her how many lovers she's had, and she counts them out on her fingers: maybe six. Then she asks him, and he flashes all ten fingers several times.

I pretended I was Belmondo and wiggled my fingers interminably. I was kidding. Marc was in earnest. He raised his index finger, then pointed at me.

"You've never had sex with anyone but me?"

"Oh," he said, correcting himself, sticking up his middle finger to make a peace sign.

"Me and one other guy? You've had sex with just me and one other guy?"

"Does masturbation count?" he said, raising his pinky.

"What counts is two guys in the room together, with something intimate out in the open."

"Oh," he said, lowering his pinky. "You didn't say they had to be in the same room."

"You've only had sex with two men," I said, phrasing it not as a question but a statement, testing its likelihood.

"Are we talking *sex*, or do you mean *love*?"

"Well," I said, "now you've run into my area of extreme perversion. Everyone I love gives me an erection. It's why I can't have dogs. And I can't tell the difference between friendship and love. I fall in love with all my friends, especially if they're hurt. I can't resist anyone who needs my help."

"Strangers on the street who ask you directions?"

"I want them."

"Can you tell me how to get to Orchard Street?"

"I'm not kidding."

"Neither am I."

"It makes a lot of people really angry."

"He was a cop," Marc said, suddenly.

"Okay, rapid transition. Who was a what?"

"The only other guy besides you. You're shocked, aren't you?"

"Not by 'cop.' I'm shocked that there were only two people you ever—"

"Not just two. The first man I ever loved was Will Robinson. 'Warning! Warning!' I wanted to be his robot." He sighed. "But if you mean *been in love*, well . . ." His voice trailed off, and he looked at me hopefully. "Just you. Not even really the cop."

"This was a cop you knew?"

"We lived together for ten years. In Philadelphia. I met him when I was at Penn. I was in Kennett Square reading *Discipline and Punish*. He sat down next to me—he was out of uniform—and said, 'I see you're in my line of work.' That was his entire comic repertoire. He exhausted it all in one sentence. I found out later that he read French theory for pleasure. He would read a hundred pages of *Madness and Civilization* and then watch a basketball game. We didn't have a lot of sex, and I was not in love with him. But we slept in the same bed for ten years. He was big, which I found . . . convincing. I was convinced by his materiality in a way I never believe in my own. I am not very tall. You have no doubt observed. I am insubstantial. Every part of him was wide of girth and rather dense."

"He sounds cute."

Marc and I had the same taste. I was starting to learn this and to feel nervous about it. I don't like mirrors. "He had an insistent pulse," Marc said, "and when I held him in his sleep, I knew that at least one of us was alive."

"Are you quoting me?"

That was when he asked what David was like.

"Oh. Um. Before he got sick, he was charming and anxious. I like people who despise themselves. It's a form of pride I get."

"What else?"

"He had a corny sense of humor."

"So does Harpo Marx. What was he like?"

Why was I having such a hard time with this? Dave's personality was quick and frenetic, and it was all laid out in front of you. He kept nothing back. He was a man who happened in a minute, and explaining him would take all day.

I shrugged. "I don't remember," I said.

"You have no comment?"

"He changed so much in the last few months of his life. When I think back, there's a blank. All he was was sick."

"You never have no comment."

"I'm sorry."

"You have comments on *breathing*."

"Breathing is weird."

"You were in love with David. Why can't you describe him?"

"Are you crying?"

"I'm not crying."

"You're cold." I pulled the sheet around him. "Maybe the air conditioner is working."

He rolled away from me, curling into a ball. "You'll never love me as much as you love him," he said. "My competition is a corpse."

"I never slept with David."

"So he'll remain a missed opportunity. The best kind. They never go wrong."

"Sweetheart," I said. I didn't know what else to say. "Everyone is disappointing," I said. I meant this as reassurance. I don't think it worked. "I'm certainly disappointing. That's why I slept with you on our first date. I want people to know right away how deeply average it'll be."

"*People*," he said. "You have *people*. I have *person*."

"One is enough to ruin everything."

"You fell out of love with David, and now you can never forgive him. How do I measure up to that?"

Was it a rhetorical question? A prediction? A dare? In any case, we broke up a few weeks later. Okay, I dumped him over brioche.

Afterward, I ran into him a few times. He had gotten a vicious little dog named Johnny Depp, small enough to carry around. There would be Marc in Tompkins Square Park, Johnny Depp trembling and outraged in his arms. A tiny dog instead of me. Dog as weapon, dog as rebuke. I knew to stand back.

Less Is Less was harder to elude. Five years after our breakup, it was suddenly everywhere: raved about, in the pages of magazines; repeatedly spun, in coffee shops and gay bars in the East Village; and in the apartments of all my friends.

For a long time, I ignored it. As much as I could. Then on a grim and grizzly day near Christmas, the shortest day of the year, I saw the CD in a lit store window on St. Mark's Place, and I went straight home and downloaded it illegally from piratebay.com. I was overwhelmed. There was our whole summer, returned to me in rhyming couplets. He had captured the heat of August, and the sound of water pipes harping the walls in dumbbell flats on Clinton Street, and the self-conscious slumming of white kids from Westchester living in squats on Avenue C. And in the middle of each song was me.

I listened to the record every day for two months. It inflamed my narcissism. So what if he called me a liar? A necrophiliac? A whore? Marc had studied critical theory in college, where his honors thesis was "Foucault, Or: How To Hide." The paradox of his fame was that he preferred not to appear, and he wrote great confessional love songs in order to remain obscure. I'm the opposite. I want to be seen, and I have a compulsive need to confide and reveal, to make myself transparent to an embarrassing degree, and to get control by giving myself away.

We were perfectly matched, the hidden and the disclosed. I was what he confessed. He showed himself to the world by pointing at me. The songs were beautiful, lovely and funny and sad, and produced to prevent their going mainstream (which is why they did anyway). The arrangements highlighted his collection of odd instruments, didgeridoos, and serpentine bassoons, and an exact clone of Ben Franklin's glass armonica. He had the integrity of being just famous enough. Not Cher-famous—he could walk unmolested in Beverly Hills. But he was known on sight by hipsters pretending they were too cool to notice him in Brooklyn or Austin or Orlando.

And I was the open secret of his songs. It's very heady to be a semiotic code. For the first time in my life, I felt hip. I'd wake up in the morning wanting to go to Williamsburg and just be trendy. I stood around the lobby of the Film Forum, congratulating myself for not being noticed, I was so occult.

"Greetings," Marc said, meeting me in his hotel lobby in downtown LA. He liked to take a folksy tone as if he were descended from sharecroppers, though his parents were both psychoanalysts who worked for the military treating combat stress. They traveled from one army town to the next all throughout Marc's childhood, from Hawai'i to West Germany, succoring and supporting large stunned men with short haircuts who cried a lot when they weren't threatening people with guns. "I grew up thinking there wasn't a difference between violence and hugging," he told *Spin*.

"Marc," I said, as always with a mixture of affection and guilt. I went towards him, then held back. At the same time, he was moving in for a kiss, and we ended up awkwardly brushing cheeks. I put my arms around him, and we embraced, sincerely and apologetically on

my part, hopefully and resentfully on his. Then I pulled away and re-
garded him, jealously checking for further signs of success.

He had shaved his head, and he looked like Foucault on his way
to a round of exemplary suffering in a San Francisco bondage club.
Dressed to counteract the Pacific light, he was a study in brown: his
eyes were brown and his boots were brown and his shirt and jeans
were shades of brown. He had gained weight, and his belly strained
against the fabric of his shirt. Awkwardly, I asked how he was feeling.

"I don't have feelings," he said, "I have cigarettes."

"I thought you quit."

"I'm trying to start again."

In the swank hotel, with its mood of reckless newness, Marc's depression seemed wrong. It was East Coast, sepulchral.

"You want to start smoking," I said.

"Yes."

"You're nervous about your play."

"Musical."

"Worried about your musical."

"Yes. Why are you feeding back to me everything I say as if this
were an intervention? Not even a good one. You forget I have shrinks
for parents."

"I'm sorry. You look tense."

"I am tense. I'm putting on a play—a musical—to which I have invited my ex, in a gesture of intimate friendship, except I forget that
my ex confuses intimacy with trauma, he thinks it isn't love unless it
reminds him of high school gym class, which is why, the second time
he abandoned me, he ran off with a straight guy with whom he can
spend many happy hours not being picked for the ball team—"

"Can we not talk about me in the third person?"

"I like you better that way. You need an omniscient narrator. Otherwise you're too implausible."

"You invited me. I'm here because you invited me." I put my hand on his face, brushing an eyelash from his cheek. I'm not sure he liked it, but he stopped ranting. "Look," I said, pointing at a wild profusion of red gladioli in a nearby vase, "the sunlight traveled ninety million miles to grow these plants that someone killed for us. Can't we be happy? I'm hungry. Let's eat. Where shall we go?"

That cheered him up. He had forgotten he was a pop star with an expense account. *I'm Sick of You* was being produced by a British entrepreneur and a Saudi prince, and they were providing unimaginable perks.

"Anywhere you like," he said, reaching into his pocket and pulling out a set of keys, which he jangled in front of me. "I've been banned from rehearsals, and as compensation, my 'handlers' got me a rental car. We can go to Venice and die on the beach," he said, and it was the happiest he had sounded so far.

✳ ✳ ✳

The second time Marc and I were boyfriends, he was famous, and I was broke. At least one of us had changed. One night after I had been listening to *Less Is Less* since noon, I ran into him at a Fassbinder film festival. (The parts of my life that seem pretentious and fake are not the ones I have invented.) We saw *Ali: Fear Eats the Soul*, which is about a German widow who falls in love with a Moroccan guy and gets punished for it by everyone, including him. "Which one of us is the idealistic lover," Marc asked later, after I had gone home with him in the snowy rain and endured the warning barks and heel-nipping of his awful little dog and slept with him in the tiny enclosed bedroom of his giant loft, "and which is the forbidden beloved?"

"I wish I looked like El Hedi ben Salem naked in a shower," I said.

"What I mean," he said, clarifying, "is that I am not ashamed to love you."

He should have been. This time, we lasted ten months. Everyone says I'm a fool for leaving him again, but I didn't want to be a band wife. Jerry Hall had once told *Vanity Fair* that the way to keep Mick Jagger was to make sure he was never more than ten minutes away from a blow job, but our difficulty wasn't with each other; it was with everyone else. When we were out with his pop star pals and artists' reps for the record company, Marc closed down like a shuttered bodega. He was mute, and I was on my own. While he moped and smoked and rolled his eyes, it was my job, in late-night sushi bars, to talk to the A&R guys from England whose questions about my life and career were addressed to me but asked in order to compliment Marc. I was their chance to show they could praise something of his.

"What do you do?" they would ask me, and I'd say, "I teach college," and they'd say where, and I'd wave that away. I wasn't going to explain Flushing to an A&R guy named Tone with a mouthful of teeth so gapped and cracked and capped and stained and jutting that you wanted to see how Christo would wrap them. Now I'm mocking him for what he couldn't help. Who knows if his parents had a dental plan? It was too bad about his teeth, but I was not going to talk to him about freshman comp. Instead, I said, "I write stuff," trying to swallow the words. And Tone smiled and said, "Brilliant," and asked what kind of stuff did I write, and I put my hand on my mouth and said, "A novel."

"Oh, cheers, mate," he said, in a booming voice that was meant to congratulate Marc, and he raised his pint of ale. "Would I have heard of it? What's it about?" And no, he would not have heard of it. I'm not saying it was a flop, but it had been published twelve years ago, and I still hadn't written another one. I said, "It's a boys' action-adventure story that ends in tears." Which was sort of true. It was about a kid who hates the world and dies of AIDS. Sales were light. Still, I could have said it was about a rock-star wife who buys a gun and blows away her husband's entourage, and Tone wouldn't have blinked. He wasn't listening for words; he was waiting for the space that came after the words, like a bad actor who goes blank until he notices the silence that means it's his turn to speak. When he got his cue, what he said was, "Marc, how fabulous."

I had many such outings with Marc and his "people." At the end of the night, Marc always picked up the check, which meant I had been comped in like everyone else. I was Marc's permanent plus-one. Then the two of us went back to his loft, and he would touch me like I was a Greek maid pursued by the gods but given unto man for just one night, because tomorrow she would be turned into a tree, or a lute, or a heavenly orb, and thereafter, in order to bathe in her glow, he would have to look up at the sky. That's how Marc touched me. Even though I was not Jerry Hall. I was not even a tired whore in thigh-high white boots, hot pants, and a tube top, sent up by the hotel management to help him sleep. I was a forty-two-year-old white guy with love handles and a novel that a woman in the *Los Angeles Times* twelve years ago had called "promising."

Marc was right; the subject of his songs was other songs. And though the lyrics quoted me—the lies I told, the promises I made, the stupid way I had said goodbye—still, the songs were not me, they were "you," a reference to the lost beloved in a million other songs. I felt gotten but erased, merged into lyrical convention, universal and therefore generic. I should have stayed with him because he said repeatedly he loved me, and he was not straight, and we had sex, and he bought dinner and took me to the movies sometimes three times a day not just to please me but because it turned out that we wanted the same thing, to be a movie, or failing that, to watch a movie. I left him the second time out of jealousy and shame because he had found a way to turn my personality into profitable art, and I had not.

✳ ✳ ✳

We were headed for a breakfast place in Silver Lake that neither one of us could remember how to find. Marc was at the wheel, and I had the map. I was happy to be in Los Angeles, with its flattening light and one-dimensional hills. I rolled down my window and felt the crisp air against my skin—not a dog's tongue lapping at the underside of your wrist, like in New York, but sea wind spiced with eucalyptus and exhaust, a dry breeze that ran its cracked palm down the length of my bare arm.

In his basso profundo voice, Marc suddenly said, "How's Biff?"

"Biff" was Marc's name for Phil, my latest—as in "most recent," not necessarily "current"—boyfriend.

"Let's not get into that," I said.

"When did we ever get into it? You come home late one night after we're together almost a year and tell me you're not good enough for me, which: a) Isn't that for me to say?"

"Marc, I'm a two-timing bitch."

"Maybe that's what I like. And: b) How am I supposed to know that what you really mean is 'I'm breaking up with you to sleep with Harry Potter'?"

"Phil is twenty-seven."

"That's so reassuring," he said. There was a pause while he lit a cigarette. He smoked a French brand. The tobacco was rolled in fine white paper and impressed with a gold logo. He took a long drag. Then he exhaled slowly, and said, "You are the definition of commitment anxiety. You can't even commit to not committing." When he got angry, his voice went lower, which was a feat.

"Why are we discussing this now?" I said. I was reaching into the back seat to grab a copy of the Thomas Guide to Los Angeles when Marc announced that he was thinking of moving to LA because everything in New York reminded him of me. "I'm *picking* up the *pieces* of my *shattered life*," he said. Marc's feelings, which he denied having, were nonetheless in italics. Ignoring him, I paged through the Thomas Guide, trying to find the intersection of Beverly and Silver Lake Boulevards.

"You left me hanging," Marc said, gesturing. The car swerved. "I kept waiting for the breakup call, but it never came. We didn't even have breakup sex. You climbed in bed with me one night, reeking of Biff—"

"Phil. His name is Phil. Philip Innocenzio."

"Hah."

"Well, it is."

"—and you climb into my bed, and you don't say, 'I want a divorce,' or 'I'm moving out—'"

"I couldn't move out. I wasn't living with you."

"You were just staying as long as the heat lasted because I had air-conditioning."

"I'm the child of frontier pragmatists, I make adjustments according to need."

"Why didn't you tell me that? Why didn't you say, 'The heat broke, I met someone who will never want me, I'm happy, goodbye'?"

"I have my moon in Cancer, I need secrets and surprises."

"Are you seriously quoting astrology to me as if it were a diagnosis?"

"Cancers are scavengers. They look for what's available."

"Biff was available? Biff was straight, you said so yourself."

"I said that much later, under duress, because you called me up and threatened to take drugs unless—"

"Unless you told me why you'd left. Or *that* you'd left. Normal people say, 'I'm leaving you.' Or they serve papers. It's crass, but it's clear. Unlike you. How would I know you were gone? You said, 'I'm not good enough for you,' in the same self-dramatizing tone in which you call yourself fat, or dying, or 'over.' It was weeks before I knew you left."

"I can't read this map," I said. Somehow we had gotten onto Vermont Avenue headed to Los Feliz. Every few blocks, a gust of wind blew a hole in the smog screen, and the flat desert light burst like a camera flash, briefly exposing the adobe front of a building or a cluster of trees. I gave up navigating and snapped on the radio. "We split up last fall. It is now almost summer. We've been apart nearly as long as we were together. Why are you still hanging on?"

"Because you promised to love me forever. But what you meant was 'In this moment, which *feels* like forever, because I have an attention span as long as a Budweiser ad—'"

"It was never a promise, it was just—"

"A conjecture?"

"An ejaculation."

"Oh, bravo. I repeat: 'In *this* moment, which to *me* is forever, because I've never had a relationship that lasted longer than an episode of *Mary Hartman, Mary Hartman*, I love you.'"

"*Mary Hartman* is a really good show," I said, as if in defense.

"Where I come from, 'forever' means 'until the earth explodes.'"

"*Marc.* Does anybody want to be loved until the earth *explodes*?"

Then one of Marc's songs came on the radio. Spun faster, his voice was a pleasant, boyish baritone. "Athena broke out of the head of Zeus," sang Marc on the radio, as Marc in the car smoked his cigarette. "But you broke my heart and snuck in." He was surrounded by versions of me in different media formats. He slowed the car and pulled to the side of Los Feliz Boulevard, admitting he was lost.

I sat still, holding the map, pinned in place by his lyrics. His songs about me said one of two things. They said, "You're beautiful and perfect, and I will always love you." Or they said, "You're cold and incapable of love, and I will always love you." This song said both. I didn't know whether to hold him or flee. There was a clinical name for my response to Marc: approach-avoidance. A mule stands between two bales of hay, and starves because it can't choose? No. Approach-avoidance is this: children are asked to perform an unpleasant task in order to get what they want. What was I getting from Marc? Endless love and radio play. And what was the unpleasant task? The same thing: being loved for all time, by someone whom I didn't love as intensely in return.

Phil's love, unlike Marc's, had been fluctuating and unpredictable. He disappeared into his apartment for three days straight and played computer poker. Or he took off to Atlantic City with his pals, accumulating cash and then spending it on lap dances. He was in Cancún right now, for all I knew.

"Actually, Phil and I aren't doing so well," I said. I didn't know why I felt like confiding in Marc. "I think I split up with him."

"Did he get a ten-minute warning?"

"*He* split up with *me*. We split up with each other," I said, annoyed. "Why are you always asking about him, anyway? 'Biff.' I don't even have a pet name for him. I like him less than you do."

"If you like him less than I do, you've killed him." Then he seemed to regret saying it. "I'm sorry," he said, touching my hand.

"Now that you've left me, I can't shake you loose," his song went, on the radio. "Your absence gets under my skin."

✳ ✳ ✳

A week before Marc called me from his rooftop, I broke up with Phil in his parked car. He broke up with me. We broke up with each other. It was a getaway car, with blackened windows and Florida plates, but Phil was no outlaw. He was just a kid in a souped-up Honda Accord who had finally moved out of his mom's house in Islip, the town whose name is a sentence. I slip. Innocent Phil, Long Island dude. He had a big square head like Fred Flintstone's, with thick black hair and brown eyes in a long face. My change-of-life boyfriend: mildly cruel and flattered by everything I told him about his charm, his beauty, and his intelligence. I like to invent guys; I don't want them to have too much to offer on their own. Maybe he was not fooled by my hyperbole. Anyway, he *was* beautiful. He had long arms from his shoulder to his elbow, and he looked great in a sleeveless shirt. That's not enough? He was a "hot guy" who was still in the room when I took my clothes off. That was new to me.

We met in an acting class—my change-of-life indulgence—doing repetition exercises. You and your scene partner would get up in front of the room and repeat back and forth to each other, ad infinitum, a simple observation: "You're wearing a blue shirt." "I'm wearing a blue shirt." "You're wearing a blue shirt." "I am wearing a blue shirt." The goal was to be in the moment. Not to jump ahead, or away, or out of the moment, not to devise a plot or build a character, not to think about how to say lines. Just to watch the other guy, and listen to whatever he says, and repeat it back to him. Or her. Or them. In my case, Phil.

I didn't pick him as a scene partner. The teacher made the match. There were twenty students in the class, and only two of us were over forty, a balding white guy with a threadbare ponytail, and me. I figured he was my fate, but the teacher surprised me. "You go with him," he said, a prison warden naming cellmates, and he jerked his head at Phil. Then suddenly, Phil and I were in front of the class, noticing my shirt.

"You're wearing a blue shirt."

"I'm wearing a blue shirt."

"You are wearing a blue shirt."

"I. Am. Wearing. A blue shirt."

"Button-down," he said slyly.

And the teacher, talking over Phil, said, "Faster, faster," clapping his hands. You could change the line of dialogue in the course of the exercise, but not unless the moment made it happen. "Anyway," the teacher said, "the words don't matter. The feeling is not in the words. The meaning is not in the words. Don't worry about the goddamned words. Just notice something. And let it affect you."

What did I notice about Phil? He was a kid in logo T-shirts and squeaking cargo pants with ribbons hanging down. A chubby teen, he had recently lost fifty pounds, and he carried his new body with an air of surprise, like an infant who has just learned to walk. I like people who aren't done. He was twenty-three years old—I lied to Marc. "Whatever, man," as Phil would say. I liked his voice. It had a resonant thrum, a husky, masculine reverb that was sexy, speedy and hollow, and scraped out like a skull.

He came to my apartment one night in a rainstorm and gave me a CD. We had graduated from repetitions, and we were rehearsing a scene from *Death of a Salesman*, where Biff and Happy sit up late in their pajamas, smoking cigarettes and discussing their parents. Maybe that's where Marc got the nickname, though I didn't tell him about Phil until much later. And Biff was me, by the way. Phil was Happy, if not quite gay. His body was shiny with rain, and he stood in my living room and shook the wet from his hair. Then he unzipped his knapsack and reached inside. "I burned you," he said. It was a complete sentence, but it wasn't over. I was waiting for him to reach the direct object. I knew it wasn't "you." Then he found it.

His hand came out of the knapsack, holding a CD. "Some music," he said. "You burned me some music," I repeated, and he laughed, getting the joke. "I burned you a little music," he said. "Postal Service. Soul Coughing. Sigur Rós. Stuff like that." He stretched his arm across the empty space between us, offering the disc. I had not told him about Marc. When he sometimes drove me to Marc's loft after class, I said I was feeding a friend's dog. "Take it," he said. He was wearing the CD on the tip of his index finger.

I looked at the disc, and it was ringed, like his offering gesture, with a corona of meaning. So I took it. I can't resist beginnings. Marc and I had already reached the cozy middle of our relationship, where we hung out in our underwear eating ice cream and watching, for the umpteenth time, the film version of *Oklahoma!* Marc said it was the dirtiest musical ever made, and we counted its transgressive Foucauldian pleasures: incest, murder, suicide, arson, stalking, masturbation, nymphomania, "and the prairie fence as a metaphor for the circulation of power. Not to mention Hakim, the wandering Muslim Other." Marc was ingenious and silly. And faithful. I felt trapped. I don't want love, I want transition.

* * *

Marc and I never got to our breakfast place in Silver Lake. Instead, we stopped at a 7-Eleven on Western Avenue for caffeine and candy bars, and then let the freeways absorb us, like characters in a novel by Joan Didion, managing our anomie and dread on highway entrance and exit ramps, surrendering to weekend traffic and the refuge of the road. Now and then, we were spilled out onto surface roads where we aimed for the closest landmark and swarmed it like tourists. We saw the James Dean statue in Griffith Park. We visited the Watts Towers and Frank Gehry's house in Santa Monica. We were halfway to Joshua Tree before we realized we had strayed too far from home. Marc got control of his fleet car, which seemed to jet forward without his input, and we circled back to Wilshire Boulevard.

An hour before the gala Saturday night opening of Marc's show, we were sitting on a bench in the La Brea Tar Pits, near a statue of an elephant trapped in tar and sinking to her death, while her baby stood at the shore crying and stretching its trunk like a lifeline. Past them was a swamp of sucking tar deceptively covered by a wading pond. Oil and methane gas bubbled up through the water.

"Shimmering surface, terrifying subtext," I said. "Los Angeles must be a Gemini."

"It's impossible to talk to you," Marc said. "Astrology! You're shallower than I am."

"I'm empty inside," I said, willing to indict myself if it helped Marc hate me. He needed a new muse, someone else to lose and lament.

"You're not just empty inside, you're empty outside," he said, lighting another cigarette. "My favorite kind of empty." And then he was crying. A cloud cover spread across the sky as quickly as in time-lapse photography, and it started, lightly, to rain. I watched droplets one by one staining the thin white skin of Marc's cigarette.

"After you left," he said, "after you left without leaving, after your virtual departure, I watched self-help TV. Twenty-four hours a day. Oprah, Dr. Phil. Cable-access AA. I followed the steps. I let go and let God. I forgave you not for you, but for me. It worked for everyone else. Angry couples from Ohio sat in leather armchairs and told each other they were moving on, while Oprah beamed. I couldn't move on. I wanted Oprah to beam at me. I wanted to take you on Dr. Phil and hear him say, 'That dog don't hunt,' while we both looked at you and frowned. Nothing worked. Everyone else in America is moving on but me. I still love you. I still miss you."

"It's not supposed to rain here," I said. "False advertising."

"Are you listening to me?"

"I listen to you everywhere I go, Marc. You have colonized the airwaves of every trendy hotspot in Lower Manhattan."

"Why don't you shop somewhere else?"

"Why don't you find someone else to, you know, 'hurt you into poetry'?"

"You could at least say you're sorry. I know that sounds prosaic."

The rain had saturated his cigarette. Only the red ember at its tip still glowed with heat. He was smoking wet leaves.

"I'm sorry," I said, though whether I had spoken out of obligation, love, or my need to hear someone apologize for things, I wasn't sure.

✳ ✳ ✳

Phil and I were in acting class all summer and well past fall, the summer I was still living with Marc, staying with him because he had air-conditioning and I did not. We put up the *Salesman* scene every week for a month, surviving withering critiques. The night our acting teacher finally praised us—"Nice work," he said, as if we were professionals—we were exhilarated, and we got in Phil's car and drove up and down Manhattan, replaying our triumphant scene and writing Oscar acceptance speeches. It was nearly 4:00 a.m. when Phil pulled to the curb on a side street off the Bowery, footsteps from Marc's apartment. We were under a streetlight whose glow pierced the car's interior and spilled over the cobblestone street, drawing a circle around us in the night. For a while, we sat silently, talked-out but still connected. The repetitions had worked: Phil and I were acutely attentive to each other. And we had learned how to "be real in the midst of imaginary circumstances," the acting teacher's instruction.

We looked at each other for three silent beats before we kissed. The kiss was the real part. What was imaginary? Everything else: that a straight guy just happened to want me; that age doesn't matter; that I didn't have a boyfriend; that Phil didn't have sort-of-a-girlfriend (I learned later); that sexual desire was more fluid than even Kinsey allowed; that it wasn't long past everyone's bedtime, including Marc's—faithful Marc, who was home in his bed waiting for me. I got out of Phil's car and walked to Marc's place. It didn't seem right to ask Phil to drop me at the door. I had a key, and I snuck into Marc's loft and crawled in his bed in my street clothes, and said, "I'm not good enough for you."

I don't cheat; I just scram. I'm monogamous until the minute I'm not, and then I'm gone. Marc thinks Phil and I were sleeping together all along, but we were doing repetitions long before anything irrevocable happened. It was nearly dawn when I showed up at his loft. His bedroom doubled as a studio, and it was jammed with recording equipment: guitars, synthesizers, drum machines, soundboards, and laptops. A mike hung over his bed like a noose, and his headboard was a foam soundproofing pad. I had to admit there was something luxurious about being fully dressed in my lover's bed, with his musical career crowded around him in the dark.

I rubbed his brow, tracing his receding hairline with my thumb. He was nestled in his flannel pajamas and blue flannel sheets, with his dog curled up near his head. Marc had told *CMJ* that Johnny Depp belonged to an ancient breed that had once been food for conquistadors in Mexico, and I pictured a Spanish knight keeping a small, rough beast at hand for loving pats and discreet nibbling on its underbelly. I thought I knew how it felt to be cuddled and cannibalized. Guiltily, resentfully, I threw a stuffed toy for the awful dog. Then I left without taking anything—my clothes, my books, toothbrush, and bicycle. That was just before Thanksgiving. My thing with Phil lasted until Christmas Day.

✳ ✳ ✳

We broke up after Christmas dinner at his mom's house in Islip. I was a last-minute invite. He met me with his car at the suburban railroad station, half past two on Christmas Day. "My stepdad is kind of Joe Pesci in *Goodfellas*," he said as I was buckling into my seat, which was ratcheted low to yo-dude slouch-height. The driver's seat was only slightly higher. "And he thinks I have a girlfriend," he said. "Which I sort of do." Everything was "sort of" or "kind of" with Phil; nothing was "really." Girlfriends, Joe Pesci, relationships with gay guys. I was struggling with my seatbelt and the perilous angle of the seat back. "What're all your passengers, constantly napping?" I said, trying to find the lever that would make the seat go upright.

"You're funny," he said.

"*I'm* funny?"

"You're funny."

"You have Joe Pesci for a dad and a girlfriend, I'm funny?"

"You're very funny."

And it went like that. We couldn't get past our repetitions. Questions weren't answered, just repeated with variations. A relationship that consisted of acting exercises, and an age difference big enough to span Madonna's career, isn't equipped to survive Christmas dinner with a Pesci-dad, a large angry dog, an anxious mom, an absent girlfriend, a gaggle of cousins, gift-giving under the decorated tree, and a forty-something white guy whose presence in the room is explained to the assembled company as: "He's my scene partner."

Throughout dinner, Phil's stepdad told gay jokes, not the fun kind, and Phil grinned and ignored me. Anybody could tell we were sleeping together because of how we never touched. I was a signifier for what couldn't be said. Phil's family was too absorbed in their compulsory heterosexuality to see that they had at least one gay man at the table. Or maybe that was how they noticed change, by pretending it wasn't there. Maybe they thought fag jokes were what queers liked.

I'm addicted to boyfriends with a hostile entourage. Marc's right: I'm trapped in high school gym class, forever looking for men who will make me feel like the gay one. I need to be the lone queer. It's a repetition-compulsion, like puking after dinner to stay thin. Or it's therapy. "Freud told the unhappy Present to recite the Past like a poetry lesson," W.H. Auden says, but Auden never had Christmas dinner in Islip. Replay the dialogue often enough, he means, and sooner or later, you'll stumble at the point in the narrative where the trouble began. That was my strategy. If I kept repeating the scene of my abjection, I told myself, eventually the script would change, and I could walk away unscathed.

Or not. Phil drove me back to the train that night, full of cheer, seemingly unaware that he had not once spoken to me in front of his family, and that we had addressed each other directly only in his car.

"Is this the deal?" I said.

"Is what the deal?"

"This," I said, gesturing with the whole of my right arm, as if I meant the wintry silence of the night, the tight, dry streets where the snow had yet to fall, the shuttered fronts of chain stores closed up for the holiday, even the Edwards convenience store blind and sealed against Christ's return.

We pulled into the Islip station. Phil left the car running.

"You're not happy with us," he said.

"'Us'?"

"You and me. We make you unhappy."

"'We' make 'me' unhappy?"

"I can tell." He put his hand on the back of my neck, which I resented. It felt good. "I noticed at dinner," he said.

"You noticed nothing at dinner."

"I noticed a lot of stuff."

"What, the string of homophobic, not to mention racist, Michael Jackson jokes your stepdad has apparently been committing to memory for twenty-five years? 'Boys' shorts, half off,'" I said, delivering a punch line, doing his dad's voice.

"Michael Jackson's not gay," Phil said. "You know better. He's a pedophile."

"That's in dispute. But thanks anyway for educating me on the difference between boy-touchers and gay men. And your mom ingeniously seated me next to your twelve-year-old cousin, who's blond and sulky as the kid in *Death in Venice*. I'm sitting with Tadzio and your dad tells gay jokes, and looks me straight in the eye. Which, by the way, was more than you did. And then Tadzio—"

"Tommy."

"--whatever, reaches across me to get the butter, and suddenly everyone stops talking at once, just long enough to hear me say, 'Can I get you the butter?' So I could, what, lubricate him? Was it a set-up? A sting? Did the whole family rehearse it? Why didn't you whack me while you were at it?"

"Now you're being anti-Italian."

"I mean, if your family doesn't know you're gay, fine—"

"I'm not gay."

"Okay, sure, please."

"That's a label."

"Stop, seriously, I believe you."

"I'm not a label."

"I said okay. Okay? Please don't tell me again that you're not a label."

"I already did."

"I can't hear again how you're not a label."

"I just told you I wasn't a label."

"I said I believed you. Phil. You're not a label."

We both stopped talking, defeated. We heard the *chuff chuff* of the engine rhythmically turning over itself, and I could picture the spit-blasts of exhaust-fume condensing like hot breaths on the December chill. Phil's hand was still on the back of my neck. He had great hands, the kind with an independent command of the physical world. Phil's hands were more self-confident than he was. I trusted him because of his grasp. Tenderly, indulgently, in a tone that was clotted with bullshit intimacy and yet which he clearly felt to be authentic, he said, "You're such a wonderful man."

"What?"

"Awesome and wonderful. And me, I'm just—"

"Half my age? Practically illegal? You're my Soon-Yi Previn?"

"You know, man: unboyfriendable."

"What? Who are you quoting?"

Actually, I knew exactly who he was quoting: me. It was something I'd told Marc when I dumped him the first time, and he put it in a song. Phil was one of Marc's fans. I was getting dumped with my own words by a guy who was quoting a song by the guy I dumped in order to be with the guy who was dumping me.

"We need a break," Phil was saying, and I almost agreed. "It'll be good for us."

Then the train came down the tracks, and Phil said, "Hurry, don't be late," and he removed his hand from my neck. "We'll talk," he said, making the universal thumb-and-pinky-projecting phone sign with his formerly grasping hand.

I got out of his car, hating myself for being there, for wanting him, for leaving Marc, and for having nothing else to do on Christmas Day but listen to fag jokes at somebody's dinner table. And I hated myself even more for what I said next.

"Don't forget to call me," I said, turning back, last look in his brown eyes before I shut the door. "Okay?" I said. He said okay. And I was alone in the suburban night, meeting a train.

Oh, there's nothing as sweet as self-loathing, nothing as constant and sustaining. It's exhilarating to be the subject of all that scrutiny. To take everything into account: your body, your actions, your taste in furniture and friends, the embarrassing noises you make when you come. Finally, you're central, essential to someone, if only your rejected self.

It was like having a soul. I was hauled up out of my body through a hole in my chest and flung a safe distance away. Standing there, alienated from myself, watching Phil drive off, I saw that this was what I had wanted: to be handed over to the wrong guy. A kid, who didn't get me.

What made me think we could ever be boyfriends? He wasn't interested in me. He was busy with voice lessons and guitar lessons and computer poker and the friends he met at the 12-step meetings he attended compulsively, AA and NA and OA and GA and CoDA and OLGA and CLA: drink, drugs, food, cards, codependence, computer games, and addiction to clutter, which is comorbid with pathological hoarding, or disposophobia, the inability to throw anything out. He knew he should get rid of me, but he wanted me around. He needed someone to neglect. I was what he liked to ignore.

And I couldn't resist his indifference. It was like dating my dad. I told him I was a writer, and he said, "Cool." Then he changed the subject. At first, I was relieved—the only thing worse than not being heard-of was explaining why you might have been heard-of. Soon, however, I was wondering why he didn't want to know things about me. He said he might be bisexual, which in my experience means, "I want to have sex with everyone but you." Maybe his sexuality was organized along a different axis from homo/hetero. I never knew what constituted the poles of his attraction. Food/not food? Praise/blame? Driving/everything that isn't driving? We sort of had sex, depending on what you mean by "sex." Or "we." Maybe his desire was not about genitalia. Maybe it was not about either/or. His world was undivided, an amorphous mass in which whatever he put in his mouth was him, and therefore reassuring.

And what about the thing where I picked him because he didn't expect much? He was a hot guy. If he were gay, he would have been entitled to a boyfriend who had six-pack abs, hard pecs, and an epic dick. But I was an average white guy. Because he was straight, he didn't know that he could have done way better. Dating straight guys was the opposite of high school gym class. They didn't mock you for your inabilities and critical lacks. They were happy enough with what you had.

Marc's musical had nothing to do with nuns and strawberries. It was a rock version of Søren Kierkegaard's *Fear and Trembling*—existentialism with a backbeat and sometimes an accordion. "They were threatening to call it *Kierkegaard: The Musical*," he said, "but I had a fit. Stick 'the musical' at the end of anything, you get an instant cheap laugh. *Broccoli: The Musical. Canada: The Musical. Oprah: The Musical.*"

"Oprah kind of is a musical," I said.

"Exactly. Everything is always already a musical, including 'always already.'"

We were at Marc's opening at REDCAT, a performance space that was slung on the back of the Disney Center in downtown LA like a chicken coop for the avant-garde. Marc and I headed down the aisle to our VIP seats.

"Their title was cutesy," he said. "Am I cutesy?"

"You're not even cute," I said. The joke landed wrong. We endured an awful pause. "Sorry," I said, feeling both defensive and repentant. "You set me up for that punch line. I had no choice. Of course you're cute."

"No, you're right. I'm not cute."

"You're not *not* cute," I said, which hardly helped. "I mean, you're really cute. Seriously." I put my arm around his shoulders, which was unfair. Even I felt teased. "Sorry," I said again. "Sorry, sorry, sorry, sorry, sorry."

We took our seats, and as the lights went down, he grabbed my hand. He sat for a while with his eyes closed and his head thrown back, but he was out of his seat and headed for the lobby at the first scene change. I saw most of the show alone. It lasted ninety minutes without intermission, but for me, it took as long as a car crash. The action seemed to go fast and slow at the same time, and I sat there transfixed and immobile, unable to move even when Marc was dragged onstage for the curtain call and given a single red rose, while the audience all around me stood up and cheered. I didn't stand; I didn't clap. No doubt it was a masterpiece, but it might have been dreck. I had no idea what it was like. All I knew was that it was not about me.

It wasn't Kierkegaard, exactly—it was the story of Abraham and Isaac told from the point of view of the sheep. Musically, it was Rodgers and Hammerstein crossed with Napalm Death when they were recording *Scum*. Thematically? Was it about Marc and his parents? Maybe it was a musical about all other musicals, though it would have taken some excavating to find, like, *Mame* in there. Was I still Marc's muse? It seemed not. Anyway, what the hell is a muse? A poet's conceit. "Sing heav'nly muse," John Milton pleads, yet the rest of the poem sounds just like him. Muses don't speak in blank verse, full of quotes from Seneca. There is no goddamned muse. Marc was the subject of his songs. Everyone he missed, whatever he lamented, was him. Even when he quoted me, it was him. Except he wasn't quoting me anymore.

✳ ✳ ✳

"I came out to my folks," Phil said. He said it fast in a crowded bar on Greenwich Street. We were on the second floor of the Spotted Pig, squeezed around a table with all our pals from acting class. It was February. Phil and I had both gotten new scene partners. We were acting with other people now. My partner was a foreign exchange student named Delilah who had run away from her parents in Manila. She was tiny and nineteen, with a tattoo of a torpedoed fighter plane spiraling into her breasts. I knew this because she wore low-cut strappy blouses in February.

Phil's new partner was himself. He was doing a monologue—an aria—by Edward Albee, from *The Zoo Story*: a guy named Jerry poisons a dog who doesn't die, only to fall in love with his victim. Afterward, he finds a married man on a park bench and confesses his love and his crime. Each week, Phil needed someone to sit in a chair while he circled him and delivered his speech. He always asked the balding ponytail guy, not me.

Delilah and I were doing a scene from Shaw's *Man and Superman*. It wasn't going well. I was Jack, her guardian, and she was Ann, my ward and secret beloved—a secret that my character kept even from himself. "I won't, won't, won't, won't, WON'T marry you," I had to tell her, stomping around the stage and pulling a petal off a rose at each "won't." "Marriage is to me apostasy," I said, "profanation of the sanctuary of my soul, violation of my manhood, sale of my birthright, shameful surrender, ignominious capitulation, acceptance of defeat." I'm ashamed to say I beat my chest. It only happened once. After our first time up, the teacher called me "Pookie." He wasn't being affectionate. I stopped hitting my chest, but nothing else changed. We had done the scene three times, and I was still Pookie, which was now my nickname. Even Phil was using it.

"What do you mean, your 'folks'?" I asked Phil. "That sounds Russian, like peasants. Are your parents Russian peasants?"

"I thought you'd be proud of me, Pookie," Phil said. Then he laughed his raspy laugh. He was developing a sense of irony. I flattered myself that he had learned it from me, but maybe he was picking it up from the acting teacher. Or maybe he'd been ironic all along, and I had failed to notice. "You were good tonight," he told me, an obvious lie.

"I sucked."

"I thought you were good."

We had tipped our chairs back against the wall in order to be private. There was no possibility of whispering in that room. It was a loud, crammed, intimate, public room in a three-story brick building with wood floors and low ceilings of pressed tin. None of us could afford to be there, which was why we picked it. It was so pricey and European that we could imagine we were rich, or British, or really actors. Or in Phil's case, gay.

Phil and I had stayed friends after our Christmas split, and we often sat together after class at the Spotted Pig. Nobody knew about our aborted fling, and not just because we had kept it on the down-low. They all thought Phil was straight. Now the straight guy with whom I had been sleeping from Thanksgiving to Christmas was coming out to me.

"Aren't you proud of me?" he said.

"Please, Phil," I said.

"You're being self-protective because I hurt you," he said. "I know that. I'm sorry. I told my stepdad I loved you. Which I do. I still love you."

I fell forward in my chair. The sudden jolt tipped the table, and beer slopped out of glass mugs onto the tabletop, which was littered with marinated olives, the only item on the menu that everyone could afford. Phil let his chair fall back to the floor, and he took my hand under the table. Nobody saw. Still, "We're in love," he said out loud, and he kissed me on the mouth. Everybody understood that it was a performance. Actors, right? Everybody but me. I thought his hand was telling the truth. It squeezed mine tenderly, realistically, even as he licked my face theatrically and sniffed my hair like a dog. Kissing a gay guy in public was proof he was straight. "I love Pookie," he said, and everyone clapped. "It's beautiful that you're so comfortable with your masculinity," Delilah told him, and then he kissed her while I watched.

And that was the start of our second act. We slept together, off and on, for another month. All we had were finales and opening numbers, often in that order, first the ending and then the beginning again, and because the relationship was always almost over, everything was either brief reconciliation or sad farewell. Is there a difference between apology and oral sex? I became a connoisseur of mournful hand jobs.

He was most into me in the Spotted Pig, where he liked to touch me under the table. His stolen grasps and glances were abrupt and passionate and over fast. Maybe he was out to his parents, but he liked to hide. Shame excited him. Am I calling him Catholic? Some people can't be themselves unless it's forbidden. I'm not saying he was a homophobe. He supported gay marriage, gay adoption, gays in the military, and openness and equal rights for everyone but him. His sexual preference was sneaking around.

* * *

I went to Los Angeles to see Marc because I wanted to be with someone who couldn't resist me.

"I think we've been here before," Marc said.

His musical was over, and we were standing at his hotel window high above Los Angeles, staring out over the city lights and across the desert to the Pacific. I thought I could see the Santa Monica pier, but Marc said it was the Staples Center. I put my palms out perpendicular to my face, like blinders on a plow horse, and leaned forward, pressing against the glass. Marc was right beside me. He had spent most of his musical outside REDCAT chain-smoking and pacing up and down Hope Street. His anxiety was unappeasable, which soothed me. Anxious people are my Ritalin.

On impulse, I bummed a cigarette. He enacted a film clip, putting two cigarettes in his mouth, lighting both, and handing one to me. I took a big drag and was instantly coughing. "Wow," I said, holding the cigarette well away from my face. "How can you stand this?"

"I smoke in gratitude for the packaging, which honestly states, 'If you touch me, I'll kill you.'" He laid his fingers on my cheek. "Why don't you have a warning label?"

"Anyway," I said vaguely. Changing the subject, I said, "You should live here. Downtown LA. In a big loft. You belong in a film-noir neighborhood."

Marc shrugged and took a deep drag off his cigarette. It was a further manipulation. We both knew he wouldn't be smoking if I were still with him.

"Can't you be bicoastal?" I said. "I thought you were loaded. Aren't your records selling like hotcakes?"

He blew a long stream of smoke. "Has anyone ever really 'sold a hotcake'?"

I turned back to the window. "Maybe they'd give you Frank Sinatra's old recording studio, and you could unmake *Songs for Swinging Lovers*, like that Thomas Mann novel where the guy unwrites Beethoven's Ninth. You could unmake all rock-music history, destroying it as you go."

"How could I live here? It's so roomy," he said, in his most condemning tone.

"I'd live here. I mean, if I were you. If it didn't matter where I was."

"It matters," he said. "Where *you* are."

Last year, we had talked about coming out here together. Maybe I could get a gig writing a reality show: *Who Wants to Marry an Adjunct Professor?* Marc could put out a bright, clean LA-produced rock disc, but with a death metal subtext, *Pet Sounds* crossed with Bloodgasm.

He reached out with nicotine-stained fingers as if to pull me close. He was about to kiss me when I felt my phone go off. I had left it on vibrate, in case Phil called. I knew he wouldn't. I had been calling him every day for the past week, leaving messages. I was his Marc. I am always either Marc or me, relentlessly seeking or unhappily sought. Is everyone addicted to extremes? How do people stay married? Surely they reach a compromise between infatuated and withholding. I never thought of Marc as a boyfriend. Boyfriends were people who fled. Marc stuck around. I was his boyfriend; he wasn't mine.

I pulled the phone from my pocket. False alarm. I turned back to Marc.

We were backlit, and our heads were mirrored in the window, and then through the window out across the night, in a double reflection. Our faces seemed to float above downtown, which was deserted. Marc's face was turned in profile, watching mine. I was looking straight ahead. Then our heads seemed to collide, and we blurred into each other.

So I slept with him. We had never had breakup sex. I felt I owed it to him. Surprise ending: he didn't want it. All we did was sleep. I'm a guy who doesn't have sex with men on two coasts.

In the morning, I asked him for a loan. Rent money. I couldn't go back to New York without it.

"How much?" he said.

"Say no."

"Just tell me how much."

"Really, I mean it. Say no."

"I can write you a check."

"I'm not good enough for you, I told you."

"Tell me how much you need."

"This proves it."

"I think you made it clear to me long ago what you're like," he said, searching for his checkbook. He was packed and ready to leave town. Katherine Mansfield was playing that night in Portland, and Marc had an early flight.

"Actually," I said, "cash would be better." I tried to make my voice very small. "I don't have a bank account at the moment."

"Why aren't you kidding," Marc said. It was not a question. "I can make out the check to your landlord. All right? Then you can give it directly to him."

"Her."

"Fine."

"Mindy. She's an architect."

"Can you spare me the colorful novelistic details?"

"It has to be cash. I told her before I left town that I'd have cash for her when I got back."

"You're unbelievable," Marc said. He got his luggage, and we went down to the hotel lobby, where they had an ATM. He withdrew twelve hundred dollars. His bank account had a high withdrawal limit. Or was it another pop star perk?

"Live in the real world," he said, placing a hundred-dollar bill in my palm. "I finally found my 'I want' song. I want you to live in the real world. Can you? Live in the real world," he said, giving me another bill. "Live in the real world," another. "Live in the real world," he repeated, each time placing a bill in my palm.

We hugged, sort of, and I followed him out to the street and waited while the hotel concierge fetched his rental car. Then I watched him drive away.

There goes my spare, I thought. I always kept an extra boyfriend in reserve, like a donut tire that'll last a few hundred miles. Now I had none.

I like the start of an affair, but even more, I look forward to its ending. The tougher or longer the breakup, the greater the relief when the guy is finally gone. Once the door slams, I settle back into myself, taking inventory of my feelings, the way you test your mouth with your tongue after a tooth is pulled. Does it hurt? Yes and no. I'm fascinated by the new space that is opened up by someone's departure. Touching it, finding its sore spots, I feel more present than I ever do in a relationship. I think: this is what I'm like, now, without him. It's so clarifying to lose things.

$$* * *$$

The last time I saw Phil, I tried to choke him in his car.

It was our last breakup—latest, and final.

First, I was on the roof of my building with my cell phone in the rain, and I was calling him, and I was saying—really, yelling:

"If you don't come here now, I'll—"

What? I didn't say what I was planning to do if he wouldn't come. Jump? Fly? Scream? I was already screaming. I was pretty sure I couldn't fly. And the building was five stories high. I had read somewhere that you had to be at least ten stories up to die from jumping. Was that what I wanted, to die? Possibly. Mostly, I wanted Phil to show up. Beyond that, I hadn't planned. "If you're not here right now," I said. "If you're not here."

He was sleeping with somebody else: Delilah. They were doing a scene for acting class. It was a big hit. He was Barney, the married schlub, and she was Bobbi, the elusive pothead, in *Last of the Red Hot Lovers*. The teacher liked how they used their props. He was always assigning scenes from Neil Simon plays because they were full of objects—handbags, gin glasses, kitchen utensils. Afterward, he would say,

"You really used the griddle." Phil was wearing my underwear the night he and Delilah got praised. I saw the waistband when he lifted his arms and his shirttails pulled out of his pants. Later, at the Spotted Pig, he kissed her in my underwear in the crowded corner near the john.

Miraculously, he came when I called. He showed up at my door in his car, downstairs, just under me. If I jumped, I would land on his roof. I thought of the Frank O'Hara poem: "You never come when you say you'll come, but on the other hand, you do come."

He had tortured me for weeks with coming and not coming. I was always waiting for him; my life was in abeyance. Then he would suddenly be there without warning, and I would have to stop everything and be with him. Intermittent reinforcement: it was how you tested lab rats.

He came in his getaway car, and I got off the roof of my building the normal way and went down to him.

"This can't happen again," he said when I opened his car door and slid in beside him. He wasn't angry, just certain.

"Okay, fine," I said.

"I can't have you calling and threatening me," he said. "That's not how I live."

"All right."

His car was running. The rain was light, and his wipers were on Periodic. At regular intervals that nonetheless surprised me, they made that dragging-sliding rubber-on-slippery-glass sound. There's no word for that sound. Lots of things haven't been named, which is why I'm not a language poet: I don't think words are exhausted. If only they were. If only there were a name for the feeling of knowing you can't live without someone who will never want you. Or wishing you had long ago dumped the guy you can't stand to lose. And now he gets to dump you. What is the name for that?

Phil.

"All right," I said soberly. "All right, fine." I was nodding.

"I mean, you were saying you'd jump."

"I didn't say that exactly."

"That's what you said."

"It's not."

"You might as well have said—"

"I never said 'jump.'"

Then he quoted me: "'I'm on the roof of my building.'"

"There was no other way to get you to come. You wouldn't have come."

"Well, now you'll never know if I would have come."

"But you came."

"Now you'll never know if I would have come without your threat."

"It wasn't a threat."

"It was a threat."

"Turn off the car," I said.

"I'm not staying."

"Don't stay. Just turn off the car."

"I'm not turning off the car. And I'm not staying."

He wasn't looking at me, and I wasn't looking at him. I was staring down the street. It was an odd street, three blocks long and only partly gentrified, which made for stark juxtapositions, a wine bar next to a Catholic shelter filled with homeless drunks. Stoned hipsters and ruined alcoholics passed each other on the sidewalk, heading in and out of separate doors.

"You fucked my scene partner," I said.

I knew my accusation was plaintive and foolish. And it was no longer my card to play. I had ruined my hand by threatening to jump—*apparently* threatening to jump. Nonetheless, I played the card. It was the card I had been dealt; I had to play it.

"She's not your scene partner," he said.

"She *was* my scene partner."

"She's not anymore."

"Anyway, you fucked her."

"I don't fuck. I don't like the word 'fuck.' It's a harsh word."

"You slept with her."

"No."

"Phil."

"Not like you mean."

"You made out with her in a bar, for a long time, with your tongue in her mouth, in the corner, wearing my underwear, while I watched. And then later, you fucked her."

"Not that night."

"So you admit you fucked her."

He sighed. "It was part of the scene."

"It was not part of the scene."

"It happened in the context of the scene."

"It's a *scene* specifically about a guy who *doesn't* fuck the girl he has invited up to his apartment—his mother's apartment—to fuck. That's what happens in the *scene*. It's about not getting fucked. So why was fucking part of your rehearsal?"

"You know what happens when you're doing a scene. How did Brad Pitt fall for Angelina?"

"Are you kidding?"

"I only mean—"

"You just compared yourself to Brad Pitt."

"Maybe I was thinking I was Angelina."

"Now you sound gay."

"You say that like it's a bad thing. You're so self-loathing."

"Oh, shock me."

"Can we just laugh?" Phil said. "I like it better when we laugh."

"You don't get my jokes."

"No, man, you're totally a riot sometimes," he said. "You're a riot when you're not taking yourself seriously, like you could never be hurt. Can you be that guy? You shouldn't get so upset."

"I shouldn't have gotten a cell phone, is what I shouldn't. None of this would have been possible on a landline. I can't threaten to jump off my bed."

"See?" he said. "That's better. I'm sorry about everything. Okay? It's clear we're not working out. You get that, don't you?"

"Yeah. I get it."

"I'll miss you."

And then, I couldn't believe it, but he was crying. Someone is always crying when I'm in bed, or on a park bench, or sitting in the front seat of a parked car. Phil cried sweetly and honestly. It was the nicest he had ever been. There was no way I could lose him now.

"Come on up," I said.

"What?"

"Turn off the car and come up. We can have sex, make love, say goodbye."

He shook his head. "No."

"Wow, I have no dignity at all. Okay, so what: please?"

Again he said no. "You always say no," I said. He told me, Well, you know, we're breaking up. I asked him if he'd never heard of breakup sex. He laughed a little. Then he dried his tears and said, "Anyway, I don't want to." And that's when I tried to choke him.

There's plenty of stuff I have left out of this account. I have changed names and events and consequences, such as how we really met, and where it all took place, and who was in control of whom. And none of it makes me look good. Not a bit of the truth that I have suppressed casts me in a favorable light. So it seems only fair at least to disclose that I wanted to shake him. Even though I didn't—didn't intend to hurt him. I was reaching across the space between us with my outstretched arms to grab his shoulders and give him a shake. At the last second, he shifted, and my palms landed flat on his collarbones, around the base of his neck. What would you think I was doing? What would anyone think? I know what he thought, and he put the car in drive and sped down the street and turned left at Second Avenue onto Houston Street, where he pulled to the far right in front of a movie theater, stopped, leaned across me, and opened my door, waiting for me to get out. Neither one of us spoke. I got out, and he drove off.

That was a week before Marc called to invite me to Los Angeles.

And it had occurred to me, when I was standing on the roof of my building with a cell phone to my ear, staring down at the pavement five stories below and figuring that if I jumped, I'd end up maimed rather than dead, and then the best I could hope for was that Julian Schnabel would make a movie about me starring Mathieu Amalric or Javier Bardem as a quadriplegic novelist who writes books by blinking his eye or pointing his chin—it crossed my mind, thinking of all the assholes I'd been in love with, not the ones who had loved me but the ones I felt I couldn't live without, it crossed my mind so late in life and even before I reached too fast and furiously for Phil in his parked car, that maybe the asshole was me.

✴ ✴ ✴

I was changing trains in LA Monday morning when he called. I could barely hear him. I was outside, on the light-rail platform above the 105 freeway, and the traffic was deafening. I had an early flight to JFK. I had risen at dawn, shortly before the subways started running, ready for the long trip to LAX, three trains and a shuttle bus. Now I was nearly there.

"Hey," Phil said.

Los Angeles traffic made a noise I had never heard in New York, a victorious windy yowl that blew away my thoughts. "What?" I yelled.

"I said, 'Hey,'" Phil repeated.

"Oh," I said. "Where are you?" I don't know why I suddenly thought he had followed me to Los Angeles. I pictured him strolling up and down Hollywood Boulevard on his cell phone, searching for me, maybe carrying a warrant.

"Home," he said. "Where else?" He paused. "I got your calls."

I said, "Okay." It was around nine o'clock in New York. He would be just waking, sitting on his puffy couch in his black boxer-briefs, eating cereal with soy milk in a blue plastic bowl. I thought of sleeping with my back against Phil's chest, his arms around me, his belly pressing into me as it rose and fell with his breath.

"All your calls," Phil said. "I saved them."

I was embarrassed, maybe horrified. My terrible calls. Apology as a form of abuse. "Forget it," I yelled. I wasn't enjoying sharing our conversation with everyone on the Green Line platform. "They have palm trees here," I said, changing the subject. "Even in the morning."

Phil laughed his raspy laugh. Marc had a percussion instrument that made the same sound. "I can't talk now," he said. "You used up all my minutes." Then there was nothing but static, and he was gone.

I missed being lonely with him. I was never lonely with Marc. Never lonely! Who could stand that? This is my "I want" song. Too bad I'm not a good actor. I have too much personality to be someone else and not enough to create the illusion that everyone is me. Acting is not about me; it's about my interest in you. I have emptied myself out in order to be in the moment with you. That's the pleasure of acting. You get to be present and empty. When you're vacant enough to let everyone pass through you, you're either a poem by John Ashbery, or you're an actor. Or you're me, in front of a room and trying not to care about words while the teacher claps.

What if the abusive narcissist was me?

The Green Line train was pulling into the platform. I did a quick travel inventory. I had myself. The body I have and am. My treacherous palms. My knapsack. Ticket and ID in my jeans pocket. I had Marc's money, which I couldn't spend. Maybe Phil would call when I got back to New York. Maybe not. He forgot stuff, which was sometimes a good thing. I don't forget. I had just enough cash of my own to get a cab home from JFK. I was grateful for what I had. Beyond that, I hadn't planned.

Political Funerals

Whole families were sleeping in East River Park, watched by the moon and midnight joggers. Everyone else was either acting up or dying out. It was the hot summer of 1993. Dave had switched HIV drug regimens from AZT to ddI and ddC and then to D4-T, which he called "Death at Forty."

We held hands at ACT UP demonstrations facing the police and at funerals.

Our friend Jon was a radical faerie and an ACT UP member, and his funeral was in Tompkins Square Park in the middle of July.

He lived a few blocks away from me on First Avenue. I used to run into him on the street. We had been arrested together. Once, we were both guests on a Jersey cable TV show about AIDS activism.

I didn't know him very well. He slipped away from you in all directions, spilled mercury, gleaming.

He had ideas about AIDS that he wrote down and xeroxed and leafleted all over Lower Manhattan. "The Metaphysics of AIDS." He said the body succumbs to HIV because it can't understand the useful information that the virus contains.

"What is he *talking* about?" Dave said. "AIDS is a UPS guy who comes to your door with an envelope you can't open?"

We carried his coffin up First Avenue, starting at Houston Street, where Karen Finley's poem "The Black Sheep" was cast in bronze and attached to a stone. Radical faeries and Jon's ACT UP affinity group, the Marys, were playing pipes and drums and chanting, "There is no end to life there is no end."

His parents had come all the way from Michigan. His straight brother from California, his gay brother from Manhattan.

The blue sky was full of clouds, and the sun cast shadows across the coffin. The pallbearers marched behind a banner with Jon's name and dates: birth, death. He was thirty-five. People held hands in a long human chain to block traffic, from one side of First Avenue to the other. At Seventh Street, we turned east to Tompkins Square Park.

The pallbearers put his coffin under a big tree. The top half of the coffin was open, and his body, down to his hips, was on view. He was dressed in a floral shirt and silky purple pants. He seemed to be staring, though his eyes were shut.

His brothers spoke. His parents stood up and recited the *Kaddish* from memory. John Kelly sang "Wigstock," Joni Mitchell's "Woodstock" with the lyrics changed, and which he sang each fall, dressed as Joni, at a drag party in Tompkins Square Park. He was out of drag today, in jeans and a T-shirt with suspenders holding up his jeans, and his feet in combat boots.

People went up to the coffin with offerings: flowers, kisses, strings of beads.

Dave and I went up.

Dave whispered to me, "My plans for my death are as follows. Everyone is getting exactly one minute to speak. And the second they mention their 'recovery,' they're done."

He was standing beside me.

He died a year later. He was thirty-eight. That's how this ends, punk-rock ending, snare drum.

Long-Term Survivors

Ladies and gentlemen, when a narcissist falls in love with you, you feel special.

      —Mx. Justin Vivian Bond
        from *Angels of the Morning: The Ladies of AM Radio*
        Joe's Pub, NYC, September 2009

The Origin of the Milky Way

My mother has walking pneumonia.

Here's what she plans to do about it:

"I'll walk," she says. "It's called 'walking' pneumonia, isn't it? It's not called 'crouching' pneumonia. It's not called 'lying down' pneumonia. It's not called 'sitting on your ass and watching Bill Maher all day in umpteen reruns until you feel like you can never for the rest of your life look at another blonde Republican bimbo' pneumonia. It's called 'walking.' You walk. Especially if you have a dog," she says. "Then you both walk. I have to. Every day, four times a day, sometimes five, I have to walk the dog. She walks, I walk, she walks me. If not for that dog, I'd never walk at all. If not for that dog, I'd be dead now like your father, and you'd have eighty-two years of my accumulated junk to wade through and cart off and sell on the street and try to fit into your tiny apartment. Walking, okay? You ask me how I'm doing: I'm walking. The dog and I are walking."

I'm tying my shoes, cell phone in the vise clamp of cheek and shoulder. How I miss the rotary phones that hung on the walls of kitchens, with their long coiled cords and thick handsets sometimes swollen with a growth of plastic meant to hold your head up while you talked and walked around the room and did what people do in kitchens.

"Didn't you read my email?" my mother says.

"Yes, yes, I did," I say, shoes tied and double-knotted. Heading out now. I look around the room for pocket stash: dollar bills, loose change, MetroCard, pens, keys; where are my keys? In a jar by the door. Cell phone's in my hand.

"If you'd read my email, you'd know about the pneumonia."

"I read your email," I say, lying. Why go through the trauma of birth if not to lie to your mother?

Keys are not in the jar by the door.

"What did the doctor say?" I ask.

"Doctor?"

"Didn't you go to the doctor?"

"I'm from Colorado, I don't do doctors. We bury our dead by the side of the wagon train and move on."

"You must've talked to a doctor if you know you have pneumonia."

"*Walking* pneumonia," she says. "Why don't you read your email? I put 'pneumonia' in the subject line. All caps. It'd take a special effort to miss it. The amount of energy you put into not reading my emails is twice what you'd spend if you just gritted your teeth and read the goddamned things."

Keys not on the desk, not on the counter next to the stove. Not on the stove. Not in my hand already or my pockets. Not in the bathroom sink. Not in the bed.

"Your brother was here on Sunday," she says. "That's how I know."

My sister-in-law is a nurse. She diagnosed my mother on Sunday. Then they took her out to dinner; Italian, my mother tells me.

The keys aren't under the bed. They aren't in my knapsack.

"So you're fine," I say.

"I'm not fine, but I'm walking, I just said."

Keys are caught in the folds of the umbrella jammed into the jar by the door. Their hiding place.

"Men don't listen," she says.

"I'm listening."

I'm listening, and I'm heading for the door, keys in hand, shoes tied, pockets filled, laptop and the Charles Dickens novel from 1841 that I will never finish reading stashed in my knapsack, which is slung on my back. The novel is *The Old Curiosity Shop*. "Night is generally my time for walking," is its first sentence. I walk down the narrow hall to the doorway and out into the light, lock the door, turn around, face the world. It's not night, it's not London, it's not 1841; it's July in Brooklyn, 2013, in front of my ground-floor apartment in a brick townhouse in Park Slope, and the sun's bright and the sky's blue behind the clouds, which are drifting and puffy and white, like me.

"I'm on my way to the train," I tell my mother.

"Fine. Hi to the train."

"I'm headed into Manhattan."

"Are you seeing Woody Allen's new movie?"

"Not right now!"

"Go see Woody Allen's new movie."

"It's 9:00 a.m. Go to the doctor. The reason you moved to a fancy condo in an expensive retirement community in Bucks County, PA, was so you could pull that cord on the wall if you needed a doctor."

"I'm not going to pull the cord."

"That's what you're paying for, so you can have a cord."

"I'm not pulling any goddamned cord."

"Listen," I tell her.

She tells me I'm the one who doesn't listen.

"Listen," I say again. "I'm at the train."

I'm not at the train. Not the train I can take. I'm at the corner of Union Street and Fourth Avenue, where the R stops, but it's not running. Hurricane Sandy wrecked the Montague Street Tunnel under the East River, and the MTA is still fixing it. Nearly a hundred-year-old tunnel, twice my age. Opened June of 1917, when the sun was in Gemini: communication, travel.

These sentimental details reverberate in my inner ear, competing with my mother's voice, as I head north to the Atlantic Avenue station at Bruce Ratner's sports arena, the Barclays Center, which is rusty and new, humped and curvilinear with a hole in its head, a cross between a giant pierogi and a bottle opener.

"You listen," my mother says, speaking slowly and emphatically. "If I pull the cord. They will send. An ambulance. They send an ambulance here if you so much as stub your toe. It's not that they care about you. It's that they do not want to get sued. I am not getting. Into. Any. Ambulance. That's what killed your father. He was alive when he got in the ambulance. When he got out, he was not. I have aspirin, and I have my dog."

"Okay," I say. "I need to go."

"Okay," she says. "Thanks for calling. See the Woody Allen movie," she says, and then she hangs up.

And I'm alone in Brooklyn.

Gowanus, Brooklyn, an ancient marshy swamp that hipsters are probably already calling GoBro. It's the flood plain that waters surge across in hurricanes.

In the distance, anchoring Manhattan, is the Freedom Tower, the tallest building in the Western hemisphere since May 10, "third-tallest building in the world by pinnacle height," Wikipedia says, at least until a bunch of towers in China and South Korea and Saudi Arabia go higher. Ironworkers from East Flatbush and Forest Hills, in hard hats and chartreuse safety vests, bolted the final length of spire in place on a spring morning while helicopters watched.

I'm watching the new tower now from a Brooklyn corner. The sky is Tintoretto blue, the color of the heavens in Tintoretto's *The Origin of the Milky Way*, where Jupiter sneaks his love child Hercules to sleeping Juno's breast, and the milk that Juno spills in surprise makes the Milky Way.

Suddenly, I need a candy bar. Behind me is the Brownstone Bagels & Bread, where the counter guy asked me once if I wanted to pay him for sex. Maybe I misunderstood. He was cute and Elvis-haired, and he called me "handsome" without provocation. I haven't been back since. Anyway, they don't sell chocolate bars.

The Freedom Tower is an empty phallus, hollow and jutting and newly done, peeking out between a Hess station and a billboard for gin. Its telecommunications peak is triangulating with the roundheaded tip of the Williamsburg Bank Building and the steeple of the St. Agnes Church on Sackett Street in Carroll Gardens. The Bank Building is set at an angle to Fourth Avenue, and so is the billboard for gin.

Everything in Brooklyn is catty-cornered and slightly askew, including me. I've got three things to do by noon. I have to pay Con Ed so they won't turn out my lights. I have to buy a liter bottle of water to take to a Queer Nation protest at the Russian Consulate on the Upper East Side of Manhattan, where two gay-guy bartenders will pretend it's Russian vodka and pour it in the street. Putin and his government are at war against the gays, among others; maybe you heard. And I have to stand in front of the Russian Consulate in a strip of pavement cordoned off by police barriers and chant, "We're here, we're queer, we're only drinking beer."

Plus, like my mother, I need aspirin—not because I have pneumonia, but because my heart won't stop beating. It beats, oh it beats, all the time. Either I'm anxious or just alive. Or I'm vein-clogged and heart-struck and headed for death, not in the way we all are, but right now on a Brooklyn corner, before I'm able to pay my light bill, which would really bug my mother.

Water and aspirin: my shopping list. I nod to the gin sign and the eight women who are dancing and painting and reading and stargazing in a mural on the side of a tenement building facing the Hess station. Then I walk to Flatbush Avenue and call my brother.

Unlike me, he answers his phone.

"Your mother says she has walking pneumonia," I tell him.

"I know," he says. "I was there. We took her to dinner. Did your mother tell you that?"

"She said Italian. I assume that means that chain restaurant place on the corner? Roman Delight?"

"Where are you?" he says. "Why are you calling me?"

"I'm in Brooklyn," I say, which sounds untrue. Before last March, I lived in Manhattan for thirty-three years. The lifespan of Christ.

"Is your mother okay today?" he asks me.

"She says she's okay."

"She was fine on Sunday."

"She's always fine. She gave me the wagon-train speech. You're mad at me."

"I'm not mad. Why would I be mad?"

"I'm sorry I couldn't go down there on Sunday. Blame Putin. You know, he's got a problem with the gays, and—there's this thing I'm doing today at the Russian Consulate, and—"

"I know about Putin. Are you getting arrested on TV? I hope you're wearing a clean shirt."

"I am, actually. Clean and new and sort of guacamole green."

"I'll keep my eye out."

"Call your mother. She sounded okay to me, but—"

"I've got someone on the other line," he says, and he says, "'Bye," and I say, "'Bye," and that's not true; I made it up. Both phone calls; they're impressions of the truth. Everything is fiction but New York. I'm not true, either. The skyline of Manhattan is true. I know the buildings are there because I watched some of them fall in real time in the actual world. Even Brooklyn is true, especially Flatbush Avenue at Nevins Street—One Nevins Street, Con Edison's Brooklyn office.

"You can't pay here," they say, when I walk in the door waving my turnoff notice at the bald reception guy and the two women in plum and aqua Hillary Clinton pantsuits behind a foldout table.

"If not here, where?" I say.

They grin and shake their heads and point to the reception desk, where a stack of flyers gives an address on Jay Street.

"How far is that? I'm new here. Can I get there by candlelight?"

Sure, I could get there by candlelight. Or I could walk, ten minutes from here to Jay Street through the Fulton Street mall.

Or I could pay my bills on time. I could pay my bills *online*. I could get direct deposit and feed my paycheck straight into my bank account and manage my finances from a PalmPilot. But I like to stand in line at payment centers and check-cashing windows, clutching my angry bill and my few dollars, or my payroll check and my IDs—passport, driver's license—waiting with New Yorkers.

For a long time in the eighties and nineties, I worked temp jobs at terrible investment banks and law firms in Wall Street and Midtown, clacking away at a Wang keyboard in word-processing centers staffed with gay guys and Black and Latinx women, the secret economic engine of the world financial market. Friday afternoons, you got your timesheet signed and ran to Tiger Temps or Career Blazers, where you traded it for a paycheck and then raced to the back of the line at the nearest check-cashing place.

Here's one way in which New York is true: it has a simple plot. Will I get to the cash window in time? Will they take my check? Have they turned off my lights yet?

I walk through downtown Brooklyn on a weekday morning past commuters and early risers and a shirtless guy doing chin-ups on a street sign. At the MetroTech Center, I feed a C-note into a Con Ed touch screen. The machine does not make change, and it gulps down my whole bill and spits out a receipt. Then it flashes a message: "Service interruption pending. See a Con Ed representative." Which means another line, another wait, long enough to read a chapter of *The Old Curiosity Shop*. Little Nell isn't dead yet. Neither am I. My heart's still beating, and suddenly I'm standing in front of a guy at a waist-high podium who takes my receipt and staples it to something else, and hands it back.

"That's it?" I say.

"Your next bill is due on the eleventh," he says.

"They won't turn my lights off?"

"Pay your bill on the eleventh."

"So I'm cool?"

He looks at me for the first time. "You're cool," he says, in a tone that means I am not at all cool, but I have lights until the eleventh.

Lights; check. Call your mother, call your brother, ask your brother to call your mother; check. Now I need water and aspirin and a train to Manhattan.

I take the A train, nearest option, under the East River to the tip of Herman Melville's isle of the Manhattoes—the financial district, always a disaster area. The Dutch show up in the harbor; it's a disaster for the Lenapes. The British get there next; it's bad for the Dutch. Yankee rebels act up in 1776; the British burn the city to the ground, from Broadway to the Hudson River. In 1835, a freak fire destroyed everything from Broadway to the East River, including the insurance industry, which fled to Connecticut, and that's why Hartford and not Pearl Street is the insurance capital of the world.

The train stops at Fulton Street, centuries of loss overhead. Shakespeare riots, 1849: an attack on working-class Irish. Draft riots, 1863: an attack on free Blacks. You know the rest. Or should. I switch to the #5 express up the East Side. I love trains; I am never mad at the MTA. When Sandy shut down the entire subway system for days last fall, I longed for its return the way Christians say they want Jesus back.

At East 86th Street, I climb to the daylight, where I find water. The woman behind the counter at the greengrocer rings up my liter bottle of Poland Spring and says, "Great book," pointing to my hand. I didn't realize I was still holding *The Old Curiosity Shop*. I'm not sure if she's asking or insisting. Should I tell her I think Little Nell is sort of a drip? Immersed in quandariness, I grab the water, smile, and flee, forgetting about the aspirin until I reach the Russian Consulate, where the Queer Nation demo is about to begin.

Queer Nation! Fabulous lesbians in charge. Spectacular omnisexuals. Gay guys schooled in the art of acting up. I don't know how I got included in the planning committee. I'm a babbler, bystander. Attendant lord, deferential, glad to be of use. Not a chief strategist. Yet there I was at a series of meetings in a conference room in an NYU building with half a dozen queer activists who were the most able, audacious, focused humans I have ever met. It was thrilling. They saw a crisis, planned an action, wrote a press release, sent it out, alerted Facebook, showed up on the appointed day with twelve to twenty activists and a huge banner designed and sewn by Gilbert Baker, and hours later it was on the evening news, looking like a thousand queers in battle drag fighting back against global homophobia.

Today's action: Don't Buy Putin's Lies!

не ведись на вранье Путина!

The choreography of resistance is specific, though its movements vary, depending on the size and complexity of the protest. There are constants, certainly at picket sites. There's a staging ground where you gather your crew, hand out signs, distribute fact sheets and flyers. Eye the police. Maybe there are a lot of police in riot gear and mounted on horseback, standing in line, holding reins and clubs. Maybe there are six bored police officers on a weekday morning drinking coffee out of deli cups.

If it's Manhattan or a city with a grid of streets or busy downtown, there's sidewalk traffic, tourists or daily commuters or habitual onlookers, sometimes penned behind police barriers across the street or down the block, sometimes walking past and reading your signs and standing in line with you at the coffee wagon that a resourceful small-business tycoon has just rolled up.

Or the protest site is more remote. Once in January, in a small town in New Jersey, for the benefit of three police officers and a shivering reporter from the local suburban paper, I lay on the pavement in front of a pharmaceutical company with my arms spread wide as if in crucifixion and linked to my friends' arms through hollow metal piping that we wore like sleeves.

Twelve of us, maybe. There was no way to get us off the ground and handcuffed and loaded into police vans without sawing through our arms at the shoulder. We chanted to the morning air, "Release the drugs; AIDS won't wait." When we got up and moved to another spot, we were a long line of conjoined t's—small "t," our heads above our spread arms.

Another time, with a couple hundred other AIDS activists and ACT UP and Queer Nation members, I got stormed by mounted police, who backed us against the wall of the New York State Theater—now the David H. Koch Theater, a reason not to go there anymore—at Lincoln Center, along Columbus Avenue.

I knew it was bad news to get near a horse who was nervous in crowds, but there was nowhere to go. We were pressed to the wall. Governor Cuomo—Mario, then—was at a benefit performance at Avery Fisher Hall, and we had come to shame him for his record on AIDS, to raise our arms in the air with our fingers pointed and chant, "Shame! Shame! Shame!"

It was nighttime, the demo was done, floodlights were shining brightly, the horses were brown, and their riders were blue, and we were pinned and lit like a mob scene in a Russian film about the revolution, while the horses' hooves made echoing sounds on the concrete.

Speaking of Russia, here's a fact sheet from the Queer Nation demo at the Russian Consulate, with news about Vladimir Putin's government:

- ▶ On June 30, 2013, Putin signed a law to arrest tourists who are "suspected homosexuals."
- ▶ On June 30, 2013, Putin signed a bill that threatens jail for Russian citizens who offend "religious believers."
- ▶ On June 30, 2013, Putin signed a bill that fines any Russian for

revealing to children age eighteen and under of the existence of "nontraditional sexual relationships."

► On July 3, 2013, Putin signed a law banning the adoption of Russian-born children by same-sex couples or anybody living in a country where gay marriage is legal.

According to these laws, Putin might conceivably arrest the Pope. And there's talk that Putin is about to sign a law taking children away from parents who are lesbian or gay, or suspected of being lesbian or gay.

That's why I'm at the Russian Consulate. Also because the 2014 Winter Olympic Games are being held in Russia, and it seems a bad idea to send gay athletes to a country where they could be arrested for saying they exist.

The demo starts. We shame the Russian Consulate. We stand, we chant, we walk in a circle. We raise our fists and look angry for photographers. We hold signs saying BOYCOTT THE OLYMPICS and BOYCOTT RUSSIAN VODKA and DRINK GREY GOOSE, IT'S FRENCH. We pass leaflets, we give interviews, we watch a pair of bartenders in red shirts from a gay bar in Midtown pour vodka into the street and onto the Associated Press reporter's "vodka cam," which is anchored to the pavement and staring up at the liquor stream.

The demo is done in an hour. Information gathered for the evening news, shots taken, reports filed, protesters inspired, workers at the construction site next to us edified or annoyed or eating lunch. Everyone packs up and goes home. Some demos end fast. "People come and go so quickly, here," I think, and I'm alone again on a corner in New York with my bottled water, which I forgot to give to the cute bartenders, and no aspirin, and still a beating heart, and my new green shirt, and a sign saying QUEERS SAY 'NYET' against a rainbow flag. The flip side says BOYCOTT THE OLYMPICS.

I'm a bourgeois pig from Brooklyn with a Dickens novel and a protest sign. Brooklyn is where bourgeois piggery comes from. So is the nineteenth-century novel, if you believe Ian Watt, whose *Rise of the Novel* I read in college, assigned by white-haired aging New Critics and the last of the Southern agrarian poets in central Ohio in 1978.

And if you believe Dan Brown, eighty-million-selling author of *The Da Vinci Code*, a novel needs a hero with a secret in his backstory.

This isn't a novel, and I'm not a hero, but here's my secret:

For the final twenty years of his career, my father, who worked nearly five decades for NBC TV, was vice president in charge of NBC's coverage of the Olympics.

His biggest professional disappointment was when President Carter pulled the US out of the 1980 Moscow Summer Games.

From 1979 to 1980, my father flew back and forth between New York and Moscow fourteen times. Then the Soviets invaded Afghanistan, and Carter bashed back. In my family, the 1980 Moscow Summer Games were code for irretrievable loss. We yearned for Moscow like Olga, Masha, and Irina in Chekhov's *Three Sisters*.

NBC had already sunk dough into broadcasting swag stamped with the network logo superimposed over the Olympic rings and the legend "Москва́ 1980." I still have some of these artifacts, on display or hidden away in my Brooklyn apartment: bath towels, ashtrays, paperweights, duffel bags, fountain pens, warm-up jackets inscribed with loss.

For a while, at least in the world of sports broadcasting, my father's name was synonymous with the Olympics, and with canceled coverage of the 1980 Games.

My father's name is John Weir.

So when I stand in front of the Russian Embassy with Queer Nation, waving a sign that says BOYCOTT THE OLYMPICS, I'm chanting on my father's grave and retraumatizing his ghost.

Is the personal political?

When my father died, I was eating dinner in Queens. My brother called. For once, I answered the phone. Somehow I knew. My brother said he was driving out to Bucks County to be with my mother, and he could pick me up in the city. Why did we agree to meet at the RCA Building, where my father worked for forty-five years? It was accidental, not conscious: neither of us was thinking symbolically. I got the F train from Jackson Heights to Forty-Seventh Street/Rockefeller Center. My father's stop. Under the RCA Building. Where his commute to and from New Jersey began and ended, for forty-five years.

I got there early. I didn't know what to do. I'd never had a father die before. A lot of people had died, but not my father. I wondered if it was wrong to wonder if I would miss him. I didn't know him. Not really. My mother, I knew. I was her gay son; she had raised me and trained me to watch her and listen to her and say what she was like.

I'm sort of her. Especially when I'm walking around Manhattan. Before they moved to their retirement community, my parents had a Jersey farmhouse and an aerie in a high rise on West Fifty-Seventh Street, and for a long time, my mother walked up and down the island of Manhattan, and back and forth across it, while my father, who had bad knees, hobbled behind her. She would not take cabs. Subway stairs were hard on her joints. So she walked. "It's good for my arthritis," she said, or insisted. If she walked all day, she said, her spine wouldn't freeze, and she would be able to get up the next day and keep walking.

I walked upstairs, the night my father died, from the subway up to the street, and put my hands flat on the side of David Sarnoff's building, the RCA Building—don't call it the GE Building, or the Comcast Building. That's blasphemy. David Sarnoff founded RCA. He was Belarusian: Давід Сарно́ў.

I stood against the building, the tenth tallest building in New York, thirty-second tallest in the USA. I thought, If my father had a soul, it would pass through here. I thought, If I had a center, it was Rockefeller Center. I stood in the portico of the RCA Building's Sixth Avenue entrance, under the glass fresco called *Intelligence Awakening Mankind*, and pictured my father walking in and out of these doors in his 1965 *Mad Men* black suit and white shirt and skinny tie.

My parents met in the RCA Building in 1953 when they both worked for NBC TV. NBC is why I'm here. It's why I'm on the planet, protesting NBCUniversal's upcoming Sochi Winter Games.

My adult life is an intervention against the media that made me.

"GAY BASHING IS NOT AN OLYMPIC SPORT," say the Queer Nation posters that I gather in my arms to take back to my apartment, where I can stash them in the closet with the "Москвá 1980" NBC ashtrays and paperweights.

My father's dead; my mother's eighty-two and walking her dog in Pennsylvania.

I'm on the Upper East Side.

I grab the posters and lean down for a discarded copy of Queer Nation's fact sheet, which you've read already, up above.

NBC is going to the Olympics, it says.

Where am I going? More protests, no doubt, but not yet. Right now, I have water. I have Charles Dickens. I set down the posters, reach inside my knapsack, and get out the bottle of Poland Spring, twist the cap, take a drink. East Ninety-First Street has returned to its daily rhythms, no longer the scene of struggle but a side street off Fifth Avenue where workers are doing construction. Later, there will be stories in the news about Russian vodka and Putin and oppressed queers. My mother will watch the TV reports; maybe I'll get another phone call. I should head home. I stuff the fact sheet into my knapsack next to Dickens, grab the posters, walk to Times Square, and take the Q train to Brooklyn, where I've got light until the eleventh.

Humoresque

"Hurts," my mother says. It's information, not a complaint. Not only a complaint. She repeats it, giving the facts. "Hurts." An accusation? She gets specific, one word at a time. "Everything," she says, in a tone of scientific precision. "Everywhere." My fault? Don't rule it out. "Hurts."

What are the symptoms? We're in Pennsylvania. She's eighty-three years old. I'm fifty-four. Last July, she had a brain bleed. A vessel leaked blood into her right frontal lobe, and the doctors, neurologists, said she would not use her left side again.

Wrong. She's been using it since August. One afternoon in the hospital, while I was trying to get her to eat the terrible hospital food—puréed hot dogs, just imagine—I watched her lift her left hand to brush away the spoon I held to her lips. That was the start of her recovery. It took weeks, then months. She slept for most of August. Did stints in two different stroke-rehab units. Learned again to sit up, slowly stand, sit back down. There was never anything wrong with her speech. She was tentative but lucid. Now she is direct and articulate as ever. "Occupational therapy," she said, "is the following. You fold laundry. Let me tell you something. I. Do. Not. Fold. Laundry. Not anymore. Ever. Been there, done that."

It's November, a week of weird weather, everything out of season, winter storm one day, spring thaw the next. Today, it's both snowy and warm. We're in the living room of her apartment in the retirement community where she and my father moved four and a half years ago. Who knows why? They stayed married for fifty-five years by spending half their time apart, my father often in their Jersey farmhouse, my mother in their Manhattan aerie. Then, in the worst housing market in the history of houses, they sold both places and moved into a two-bedroom apartment in a Philly exurb where nobody, not me or my parents or my brother and sister-in-law and their three kids, nor my sister and her family out in California, had ever been. An hour from downtown Philadelphia on the commuter train. More than two hours to the 30th Street Station from my Brooklyn apartment. Three-hour trip, door to door. Three hours also for my brother when he drives down from upstate New York.

They packed up their stuff from two homes, gave half of it away—uncharacteristically telling my siblings and me, "Take whatever you want"—and settled into their new place. Where my father promptly died, sitting out on the tiny patio with my mother, drinking a Scotch, and watching the sunset, six months into their new life. Ruptured aorta. Dead in ten minutes. Leaving her alone with the dog. A few months after his death, she fell down and broke her hip. Then last July, the stroke, brain bleed. Then rehab, then back into their—now just her—apartment, and a return to "independent living," the phrase used by the social worker and the staff at the retirement community's rehab center, where she spent six weeks.

She's home now. She's got her dog back, a greyhound named Sukie Tawdry, her true love, who stayed with my brother last summer and most of fall. Sukie Tawdry is a character in *The Threepenny Opera*. You've heard her name in "Mack the Knife," Bobby Darin's hit, number two on *Billboard*'s pop chart the year I was born. My mother hates Bobby Darin, but she likes to name her dogs after characters in musical comedies. When I was growing up, we had Luisa, Dulcinea, Eliza Doolittle . . .

Bitches. She said she would only have bitches. "Witches and Bitches" was the name of the lunch group she entertained once a year for forty years, in Jersey. She and her best girlfriends would get together with their dogs on a summer afternoon to drink bloodies and vodka *tons* by the pool and keep arguing, for decades, about Gene McCarthy and losing Democratic presidential campaigns. "Eisenhower for President, Stevenson for dinner," my mother said, and still says. She likes to tell the same jokes repeatedly for years and expects me to laugh each time.

My mother is a movie star without a movie to star in. She is the brightest, quickest, most alert person I have ever met. She never stops talking. She doesn't need sleep. Grace Kelly crossed with Elaine Stritch: 1950s blonde and beautiful, with an instinctive grasp of whatever you like least about yourself, and great skill in using it against you. Your shame launched at your soft gut, human shrapnel under your skin.

I've never known anyone more powerful except her mother, my Denver grandmother Alameda, or Ada, a steely WASP named for a Denver street, whom we called Granada. She hated Granny or Grandma or Gran. Granada was the right name. She was a grenade.

Western women, Coloradans, miners for nuggets of pain, shameful secrets. I share their intuitive knack for knowing, without being told, what hurts you the most. To exhaust my skill, I use it against myself, a narcissistic deployment. It keeps me curled in my shell and feeling singled out for attack.

My mother hates children, Republicans (two exceptions: her father, and Dwight Eisenhower, with whom she danced at the Denver Country Club in 1952), Andrew Lloyd Weber, MGM, John Wayne Westerns, the Internet, and the food at her retirement community. Also God, sports, and shopping. "Jesus and Walmart, that's all they talk about here," she says. "And little kids who visit on weekends and shit in the pool. Children are awful. I'm sorry, I know you're my son. But I don't. Like. Children. Never have. I liked you when you hit twelve. More or less."

"More or less liked? Or more or less twelve?"

"Are you blaming me? I never blamed my parents for anything. Should I not have had you? I had you, you're here; you can thank me for that. Your pleasure and pain, whatever you do with your time, your hopes and dreams; you can thank me for all that, whether I liked you in 1964 or not. So what if I hate children? Do you?"

"Do I what?"

"Hate children?"

"I can't answer that question. Some of my best friends are children. I don't want to insult them."

"You don't have any children."

"Well, no."

"You don't have anyone."

"Thanks for that."

"Get a dog," she says. "They don't hit twelve and start smoking pot in their bedroom."

"I was thirteen."

"Why don't you have anyone?" she asks me, and then she says, "Rub my feet," and I pull off her socks, slowly, carefully, and she goes monosyllabic and says, "Hurts," and "Hurts," and I don't know why I love her. It's not true that I don't have anyone. There's her. And lately, there's a guy I met last spring. He's in Pennsylvania too, nearly three hours north of here. Oh, it's complicated. Everyone I shouldn't love is in Pennsylvania. That's a song.

"What hurts?" I ask.

"Everything."

She's on the red couch that I jacked up a few inches higher the day before she got back from rehab, so it would be easier for her to lean down from her walker and sit. The dog is curled next to her. The dog is my inheritance, my mother tells me—the dog and a pair of mission oak chairs that she has carted from house to house around the country since she left Denver in the early fifties.

"I want to outlive my dog," she says. "That's my rehab goal. Every day in rehab, they gave you a goal. 'What's our goal, today?' they asked, first person plural as if I were a hockey team. 'Our goal is to get me out of here,' I said. They meant—the physical therapist meant, her name was Donna. She had Dobermans. I hate Dobermans. I knew only one nice Dobie, in San Francisco, the year Joan Crawford filmed that movie down the block from our apartment. I hate Joan Crawford. A guy at the TV station where I worked as a camera operator had a Dobie named Jack London. They hadn't cut his ears or cropped his tail. The dog, I mean, not the guy. I forget his name, the guy's name, but I remember the dog's. What does that say about me? Don't answer that. They said—you thought I'd lost the point, didn't you? I haven't lost it yet. Everything else is gone, but I still have my marbles. That's a song. They said—*Donna*, the physical therapist, said—'No, I mean, 'goal' as in, do repetitions of this exercise.' And I said, 'I know what you mean.' And she said, 'What's our goal? Thirty reps? Twenty reps? Set a goal for us.' And I said, '*My* goal is to outlive my dog.' Bang. 'That's my goal. Now you tell me yours.'"

I'm at her feet, on the carpeted floor. "You want me to tell you my goal?" I say.

"Not, not you. You rub my feet. That's your goal."

"Your goal is thirty reps; mine is your feet. What's Joy's goal?" I say.

Joy is her home health care attendant, sent by the agency. She's twenty-three and lives in Northeast Philadelphia, where she moved from Liberia five years ago. Her goal, five days a week, Monday to Friday, 7:00 a.m. to 7:00 p.m., is to make sure my mother doesn't fall. I'm here most weekends, often Friday to Monday, but today I came down unexpectedly in the middle of the week, and Joy is taking a break, sitting in one of the mission oak chairs and texting her boyfriend.

Everyone in my mother's house has someone in Pennsylvania they shouldn't love.

"Joy," I say, "do you have a goal?"

"Joy's goal is to stop treating a cell phone like a relationship," my mother says. "Is he going to marry you?"

"No," I say, thinking of the new guy up north, "he's not," and Joy laughs and pretends to be shocked because she thinks I'm talking about her.

"I haven't asked him yet," she says, and my mother says, "Don't ask him. Tell him."

"Does that work?" I say.

"Of course it works," my mother says. "Men don't listen, and they will never do what you want. Fortunately, they're also stupid, and if you tell them what they want often enough, they will eventually believe that it was their idea to want it."

"Is that your goal?" I ask my mother. "To tell men what they want?"

I'm at her feet, and I have my goal. Two goals. Her feet and her car. I need an excuse to leave early in her car, so I can go see Scott. Scott = the guy up north. He invited me to his house tonight, our first sleepover. My mother doesn't know about him, and I don't intend to tell her. Some things mean too much to discuss.

"Get him to marry you," my mother says, lecturing Joy. "Not that marriage means anything, personally. Legally—that's how it matters. For your protection. Who cares about marriage? Nobody cares. But if you die, or I die, or he dies," she says, but she doesn't finish the thought.

Joy laughs. "I'm not dying yet," she says. "Neither are you. That would look terrible on my record. But it would be worse if you fell. The worst thing for me is when a client falls. Death would be better for me."

Joy is not being ironic. She's stating facts.

"I'll try to remember that," my mother says.

"You can blame me if you fall," Joy says. "But you can't blame me for your death."

"Unless I die from boredom watching you text your boyfriend. Who will never marry you if you keep sending him irritating messages. I would not marry you either. Hurts," she says, suddenly, sharply.

I have her right foot in my two hands. "Sorry," I say. "Where?"

"Everywhere, I told you. What part of 'everywhere' is obscure?"

I'm moving my hands up her calf, carefully. She has stick legs.

When she got back from rehab, her feet were swollen, but the swelling went down. Her legs are bony, and her skin is dry. "Here?" I say, squeezing lightly just above her heel, then higher, then higher. "Here?"

"Yes, there."

"Your feet are cold."

"I know."

"Are you cold-blooded?"

"I might be."

"Are you a lizard?"

She's happy now. "Yes. I think I'm a lizard."

"Okay, lizard," I say, "I need a favor."

"You can't take my car," she says.

"Did I ask for your car?"

"Your tone asked for my car."

"I need to make a quick run, to, um—"

After all, it's a game. I've been driving her car since July. Every time I see her, every weekend, Sunday night, we do this: "Today, you will take the train home. I want my car." "You can't drive it. You're not supposed to drive it." "I will drive my car."

"You can't leave here in my car until we've had dinner," she says, compromising.

"The thing is, I'm expected somewhere in like two hours—"

"Get your lies straight before you tell them," she says.

Joy looks up from her texting. "I was just saying that, exactly."

She holds up her phone, which her boyfriend sold to her. That's how they met. He manages a Verizon store in Philly. If I'm ever on Arch Street, I should stop in and say "yo." "Yo" is my word, not Joy's. She speaks Bassa and English equally rapidly and fluently, whereas my mother and I are stuck with misunderstanding each other in English.

"I have to be back in New York for a meeting," I lie. I sound like my father, who was always leaving the room to get in his car and go to a meeting. "If I leave here at four, um. And I'll come back in the morning by the time Joy gets here. I can make breakfast."

"Breakfast sounds good," Joy says. She refuses to eat meals in any of the retirement community's five dining halls, which is how she has earned my mother's respect.

"She can't eat the food here," my mother says proudly, and Joy makes a face and says, "It's really no good."

"Back in the morning," I say, "breakfast for three."

"I'm thinking about it," my mother says.

"It's a good idea," Joy tells my mother. "We'll have a good breakfast. And then you can call my boyfriend and tell him what he wants."

My mother laughs for the first time all morning. Joy's only drawback, in my mother's eyes, is that she does not have an encyclopedic knowledge of old movies. My mother's idea of round-the-clock home health care is someone who can talk to her about Ida Lupino at 2:00 a.m. Me, in other words.

✱ ✱ ✱

Last night, we watched Joan Crawford in *Humoresque*.

"Joan Crawford made one good movie," my mother likes to say. "One. Good. Movie. Only one."

I know which one. I have known for fifty years the names of all my mother's most hated actors, why she hates them, and the one good movie each of them made. I know the only good movie John Wayne ever made. (Wayne = "Republican war hawk who is afraid of horses and pretends he isn't.") I know the only good movie Deborah Kerr ever made. (Deborah Kerr = "prissy hypocrite pretending to be a virgin.") I know Greer Garson never made a good movie. (I agree.) I know the only good movie Kirk Douglas ever made. Well, three movies, actually.

We have a routine about Kirk Douglas. My mother will say, "Kirk

Douglas made one good movie," which is my cue to say, "*A Letter to Three Wives*," and she says, "Right," and I say, "What about *Lonely Are the Brave?*" and she says, "Okay, two." And then I say, "*Paths of Glory*," and she says, "Three." And I say, "*The Bad and the Beautiful*," and she says, "Kirk Douglas made more good movies than I thought. But they weren't good because of him."

I learned that dialogue the way other kids learned their catechism.

Humoresque is the one good movie Joan Crawford made. She plays an alcoholic New York society lady in love with an idea: spiritual transformation. Passion as transcendence. John Garfield, in other words, who plays a huffy young concert violinist. "Bad manners, the infallible sign of talent," Joan says, the night they meet, at a New York cocktail party. She's rich, he's brilliant, and they both have the right lighting, thanks to Jean Negulesco, the film's moody Romanian director, and his cinematographer, Ernest Haller, who lights Joan in close-up as if she were a Norse myth. She has a perfectly symmetrical face and no subtext. Scott Fitzgerald said watching Crawford go from happy to sad was like throwing a car in reverse and abruptly backing up: you heard the gears grind, saw the tire tracks on the blacktop.

At the end of *Humoresque*, Joan walks into the sea and drowns, while Garfield, miles away in a concert hall, plays Wagner's "Liebestod." "*Ertrinken, versinken, unbewusst, höchste Lust.*" Drink up, sink down, lose yourself in the sexy waves, moonlight glinting off your Adrian gown. That's the Joan Crawford translation of the last-act love-and-death aria from *Tristan und Isolde*, which swells loudly in the background while Joan takes her life. Takes it like a drink from a cocktail tumbler that shatters when she flings it at her reflection in the beach-house window, her face splintering in close-up shortly before she gives herself to the sea, clutching a program from Garfield's concert, which she has skipped because she would rather sit home alone, drink, and die.

✳ ✳ ✳

My mother and I lie on her bed, watching Joan love and drown.

✳ ✳ ✳

"Feel better?" I say, next day, at her feet, in the late fall light, while Joy texts and Sukie Tawdry twitches, chasing squirrels in her sleep.

"Who are you meeting?" my mother says.

"*Whom*," I say, correcting her. Another of our games, fixing each other's grammar. "A game of being constantly wrong with a priceless set of vocabularies": Elizabeth Bishop.

"Smart-ass," she says. "*Whom*. Are you. Meeting."

"It's just a meeting. You know, people in a room. Saying dull stuff."

"Fine," she says. "Take my car. But if you're not back to walk the dog—"

"I'll be back."

"If. You. Are. Not. Back. *In time*. To walk. The dog."

"What? It won't happen. What could happen?"

"Everyone will be sorry," she says. Then she says, "Ow, careful," and jerks her feet away, though I'm hardly touching her.

✳ ✳ ✳

Last spring, like Joan, I fell in love with an idea, and the idea's name was Scott.

I met him online. Not on a dating site. Not Match.com, or JDate, or Manhunt, not Grindr or Scruff—"Gay Guys Worldwide" ready to hook up with you; what could be more overwhelming?—but a site for long-term survivors of AIDS. Romantic stuff. Survivors, in particular, of the first fifteen years of the global AIDS crisis, 1981 to 1996, from the first reported cases of young gay men dying of pneumonia and a rare form of cancer in New York and California, to the development, release, and marketing of a lifesaving drug regimen, HAART, highly active antiretroviral therapy. Sound technical? It's small talk on a website for long-term survivors of HIV/AIDS.

"Long-term" = Not dead yet. "Survivor" = My friends died and I didn't. Or: I should have died and didn't. Or: in 1984, I figured I'd be dead in five years; who didn't? And so forth.

Not everyone on the site *had* HIV, but we were all *living with* HIV. That was the message. Millions around the world had been transfigured by the losses they endured before there was an effective treatment for HIV. Millions still had no access to lifesaving drugs. More than five-hundred-fifty thousand people worldwide were dead from AIDS by 1996, and more Americans than had died in Vietnam.

Step on a land mine, end up hanging shattered from a tree; it would be a quicker death, but no less gruesome than deaths in the first fifteen years of the global AIDS crisis. More than thirty million people worldwide have died of AIDS-related causes since 1981. Why shouldn't fiction include grim facts? *A Journal of the Plague Years.* If Daniel Defoe were alive now, he'd be on a Facebook page for longtime AIDS survivors, collecting data, gathering impressions.

Scott showed up one day on the survivors' site—he wasn't "Scott" yet, his screen name was "Batman"—words tumbling out of his head and onto the screen in an irresistible rant, part "Hold me," part "Fuck you," a combination I can't resist.

And now I'm writing about him, which is a good way to lose him.

Some things are too important to discuss, and I've already lied about Scott. His name isn't Scott, for starters. His screen name wasn't "Batman." He has never said, "Fuck you." Or "Hold me," either, actually. I found a jacket at a Brooklyn thrift store with SCOTT sewn over the heart in script I'd learned in third grade. I'm wearing it now. It's a purple high school letter jacket with fake leather sleeves and the word FARMERS stitched in purple on the white underside of the collar. So

I'm calling him "Scott." Because there is a guy. I don't want to steal his life, though. He's incredibly tender and tall. That's all I'll say about him.

I don't want to lose people anymore, even if only in writing.

I've always liked the name "Scott." Scott Fitzgerald. Randolph Scott, Cary Grant's 1930s Hollywood boyfriend, six feet two inches tall and grizzled and reluctant in seven Budd Boetticher Westerns from the 1950s: *Ride Lonesome*, released the year of my birth, a revenge tragedy that opens in a canyon and ends with a burning cross in the desert. Scott plays a character named Brigade.

Scott Brigade?

Let's call him that.

✳ ✳ ✳

I met Scott Brigade last winter on a site for longtime AIDS survivors. After I read half a dozen of his posts and rants, I sent him a private message. "I hope you're writing a book," I said, which is a terrible thing to say to anyone. But he wrote back, and we started a friendship the way people did in the nineteenth century. As if we lived, like Virginia Woolf, in "a very communicative, literate, letter-writing, visiting, articulate, late nineteenth-century world."

"The long friendships that began by letter in those days," Eudora Welty says about the 1930s. Our letters weren't stamped and sealed with wax imprinted with our insignia and slipped through a slot in the door. Still, they made an impact. Scott's rants were bop prosody—Neal Cassady's letters to Jack Kerouac, as Neal raced back and forth across the country from Denver to San Francisco to New York . . .

His private messages, emails, status updates, texts, created him for me. Brought him to life, and into my life, as marks on a glowing screen.

My sideburned hero of the snowy West.

He didn't have sideburns. There wasn't snow where he lived, and it wasn't West; it was west of the West, coastal California. He was out there last July, while my mother lay in her hospital bed. Got into his truck with eight cats and fled the coast. Sun in Leo; inevitably, he had cats. He found them by the side of the road, hurt, limping, starving or bloody, and he resurrected them, St. Francis of felines. They were all tomcats with playground names: Bill, Kenny, Fritz, Joe, Ricky, Alfredo called Al, Manuel or Manny, and Bob.

He put the cats in his truck, and his few belongings, including his cell phone, which he never answered, and his laptop, and he started driving east—not to me, but undeniably in my direction. Though not to me. He drove for most of a month, sending updates from the road. I read them in my mother's hospital room. I don't know where the cats slept at night. He didn't stay in motels. I pictured him on a horse blanket with his Western saddle for a pillow, sleeping at the rim of a butte in Jaw Bone Flats, North Dakota, with wounded cats in a corona around his head.

Driving fast, reverse American dream: leave California in order to light out for New Jersey. He stopped just before he reached the Delaware River and settled temporarily in a tiny Pennsylvania town, three hours north of my mother's retirement condo.

* * *

I left my mother's apartment in the late afternoon, after walking the dog, and promised to be back in time to make breakfast. Waved goodbye to Joy, told my mother that she had to eat, never mind the terrible dining-room steak so tough she might be eating her cowboy boots.

I got in her car and headed for the Delaware River, where a narrow road follows along the riverbed and the shoreline path where mules in harness once pulled barges slowly downstream. I was going upstream, to Scott. Google had given me directions involving side trips through country roads that shot precipitously uphill and then down to the interstate, which connected to a series of highways that drifted into one another, each named at least three times—33 was 209 was 80—each often taking me miles in the opposite direction from my destination, because sometimes you have to go a long distance out of the way in order to come back a short distance correctly . . . Edward Albee said that.

It got dark. I was meeting Scott in a quaint hotel in the middle of town. He would be there waiting for me. I prayed the car wouldn't fail. I had never spent the night with Scott before. We had never eaten dinner together alone. I hadn't seen him in two weeks. I hadn't seen him in real life more than six times. We'd never hung out together for more than two hours. I had no idea what he did for money or fun. We decided ahead of time not to have sex that night. Somehow we both understood that whatever was happening between us was going to take a while. Fine. I've had plenty of sex. I've had boyfriends, with each of whom sex started at once. And I don't have those boyfriends anymore. Try something new. Anyway, I was twenty pounds overweight. Anyway, I hadn't been tested for HIV or any sexually transmitted infections in three years. Anyway, I hate condoms. Anyway, he was so intimidatingly, mythologically articulate, and handsome that I would rather have voted Republican than take off all my clothes in front of him on the first real date. If that's what it was.

Anyway, everyone in this story has HIV. Me, him, my mother, Joy, the eight cats, my mother's dog. Let's assume we've all been infected for more than twenty years, and some of us are struggling with compliance. How to keep taking those drugs every day. Despite the nagging routine, the side effects, what they do to your soft tissues, liver, kidneys, bones, heartbeats, over time. The expense. Permanent ties to the pharmaceutical establishment. Lifelong need for a bad job in order to get minimal insurance. The yearning to take a drug holiday, live carefree for a few weeks, get your erections back, your mood swings recalibrated, feel ordinary, uninfected—the paradox of HIV treatment being that sometimes it's when you're not taking the drugs to control the infection that you feel like you don't have it.

I have learned, in thirty-five years in New York, to assume that everyone I meet has HIV unless I'm told otherwise. I'm asking you to live in that world, where HIV is the given of the place. Make whatever adjustments you need. Just so you know.

* * *

It was dark, not moonlit, when I reached Scott. He was sitting in the hotel dining room, in his jeans and work shirt, and his bearded face, at a booth in the back, leaning against the wall, his legs outstretched, with a glass of wine. He stood up when he saw me—slopingly, from his shoulders—and laughed and put his arms around me, and we hugged, and he said my name in his soft sandpapery voice, both my names, first and last, and we held each other a beat longer than straight guys would, because it was a Republican town, and we wanted to make a point.

He smelled like trees. He was covered in cat hair. I've never had a boyfriend who was taller than me. We didn't know each other at all. I kissed the side of his face. He had thick hair; he was obviously a horse. I looked down to make sure he wasn't wearing horseshoes. His eyes were *della robbia* blue, blue of the robe, the blue of heaven's gates. I better shut up now. His pupils were contracted and small and black. We had dinner and went outside, out the side door of the hotel to the narrow street of the small town, and I got in my car, and he got in his truck, and I followed behind him to his house, which was off the bend of a long road going up into the Pennsylvania woods, and I couldn't. I couldn't believe my luck. That's what I was thinking. Luck isn't always your friend. I don't mean good luck, I mean luck as a category, like weather, or economy, or health.

"I can't believe my luck," I was saying to myself, not happily. Not *not*-happily. Because what could happen? He had no past. Not that he told. He was fifty years old. He lived hours away. We had both watched a lot of people die. They were always in the room. Their memory, their ghosts. "What could happen," I thought, and it wasn't a question. Anything could happen. I knew him as words on a page, a lit screen, and he was real now, word made flesh. He was here and actual when we reached his house and got out of our cars, and we would both die anyway, sooner than we thought or—worse—later. There was nothing but loss. Whatever else happened, that's what we could promise each other.

I haven't mentioned his hands. The hair at the back of his neck. I haven't said he's a teenage girl crossed with Elvis, if those are different things. I haven't said he has cried every time I've seen him or that I've cried. I haven't shown you his cats. Some are black. Some are orange. One has really long hair. Two of them are missing tails, maybe by accident. One has just three legs, one's got only one ear, like Van Gogh. I've never met so many tragic cats. They slept with us. We slept in his bed. He was in two layers of clothing. Sweatpants over long johns, two T-shirts. It was not that cold outside. I've never felt safer in my life.

✳ ✳ ✳

In Woodglen, New Jersey, in the early 1960s, after I got home from school—kindergarten, first grade, second grade—my mother and I sat on the couch in the living room, and I combed her hair with a blue comb, and we sat in front of the television set and watched old movies.

Gritty Warner Brothers movies. Bad guys who were really good but made criminal adjustments to manage their lifelong bad luck. They were Irish, they were poor, they were Italian peasants in New York and Chicago. What could they do but buy a Tommy gun and jump in a Model A and blast out your storefront windows? Plate glass shattered, and they felt like their luck had returned.

Or they were smart, hard women you would like to get drunk with. Who wouldn't care if you were a fag. Who didn't want you anyway. Who didn't want to be held as much as they wanted to get what they had coming to them: Bogart. George Raft. Jimmy Cagney was pretty as a girl in early 1930s movie-star eye makeup. He batted his long lashes and moved across the screen like a superluminous tau neutrino. Not a man but a particle, faster than light, beautiful and exploding. If you could slow him down, maybe you could get him to want you.

My mother taught me that Joan Crawford was not an actor, just a star, whereas Bette Davis was an actor *and* a star. It was a moral lesson. Right from wrong. The ethics of taste. "Not that Crawford doesn't have an awful magnetism. Try to turn away from her. Try to turn away from a Sherman tank as you stand there, not believing it plans to crush you. *I* could always turn away. Most people. Can. Not. Most people. Are idiots."

I combed her hair, and we watched *Dark Victory*, Bette Davis stumbling blind and ready to die up a flight of stairs, saying goodbye to her dogs, while her BFF Geraldine Fitzgerald cries off-screen, and Max Steiner's music swells in the background. "Either Max Steiner is going up those stairs, or I am," Davis said, just before they shot the scene. She lost. They both went up.

I combed her hair while Bette Davis died. She died of TB or peritonitis or a brain tumor or a silver dagger to the heart, or a car crash, or a boating accident. She lost the man she loved, or the daughter she denied, or went blind, or went mad, or went to jail, or rode with her married lover to the island quarantine, or killed her lover, or stayed a loveless queen, or a loveless teacher, or lost her lover to the priesthood, or lost her lover to the North, or lost her lover to his wife, whom he murdered before killing himself.

How will my mother die?

How will Scott die, how will I die?

I combed my mother's hair, which was blonde and thick. She would not have been a Warner Brothers star; she was tough enough but too pretty. She was a Hitchcock blonde, beautiful and chilly—a beauty she resented, though she understood its uses.

She has stopped coloring her hair since the stroke, and it has gone back to gray.

Scott has thick gray hair, wiry and water-resistant. "It's like a waterproof parka," he says. "You can pour a bucket of water over my head, and my hair won't even get wet. Maybe I'm a duck."

✳ ✳ ✳

I'm driving south through Pennsylvania in the morning light, leaving Scott's house, down Route 33. I've never been here before, though I grew up forty-five minutes away, across the Delaware River. I'm in the great valley of the Blue Ridge mountain range, the Poconos around me, passing billboards for ski resorts, Blue Ridge, and Camelback. I skied at Camelback once when I was twelve. So I'm wrong; I've been here. The part of my life where I went to ski resorts in Pennsylvania and Vermont is so remote that it feels occult, sealed from public view for a hundred years like Jackie Kennedy's blood-stained pink suit, which is stored in an acid-free container in a secret room where the temperature is permanently sixty-eight degrees.

My past is in a sealed room in another century, and I'm in my mother's car, hurrying home through a dun expanse of Pennsylvania. Snuck out of a man's house before dawn. Got in my car, backed up to his door, ran back inside his house, a straight shot from the front door to his bedroom, stumbling through the unfamiliar dark like Bette Davis discovering her brain tumor is back, found his bed, hugged him, said, "Goodbye, Scott," like how many women saying goodbye to men they planned to lose, sooner or later, in one film or another?

I can see the mountains in the distance and the scurf and scruff of gravel-peppered November snow along the shoulder of the highway. The radio is tuned to a college station. Stroudsburg.

Radio stations are awful. Since the end of summer, all fall, and now into the chill of oncoming winter, I've been in my mother's car, with or without permission, driving around New York, New Jersey, and Pennsylvania, the mid-Atlantic states of my childhood, listening to radio music turned up incredibly loud, the windows rolled down in heat or cold because I can't stand being shut in, groggy with the blasted warmth of the car heater or stifled by the air conditioner.

On the radio, a band named the Subdudes is singing a song called "Why Do You Hurt Me So?" The lyrics are basically the song title, repeated over and over. Anyone can write a song! I'm writing a song in my head. I'm a songwriter now. "Hurts." That's the song. "Everything, everywhere, hurts." Eighteen-year-olds will buy it. Eighty-three-year-olds. Gay men. That's everyone I know. What are the words? Do I need more words? No; words don't do their job. Stick to a few. Say them a lot. "Why." "Everything." "You."

Scott. Let's end this story with Scott. Pick the loved one, follow desire to its source as we head south, into the cold and slowly out of the cold. Head back down to the flat land along the Delaware, follow it home. Turn the radio high, listen to pop songs. Accusations and complaints. "If our love is," the radio sings. "We are never." "Why do you?" Better not to have too many words.

Scott is asleep in his bed. I'm not in love with him yet. Not really. I'm fifty-four. I know better than to love, too fast or at all. Do I? That's a lie; the opposite will happen. I'll fall in love with him tomorrow, and it won't go well. No; I've been in love with him since last summer. Since last spring. Since the first warm day in May.

He's here at the end of the story, sleeping with his wounded cats.

Pennsylvania is the shape of a rectangle, a page ripped from a newspaper, badly ripped at its eastern border, where the torn edge drags in the Delaware. Scott and my mother live along that ragged line. The Northern Appalachian mountain range, with its "psychographic provinces"—Allegheny Mountains, Blue Ridge Mountains, Poconos—gobbles up most of the state. Scott is high in his mountain aerie, my mother swamped in the drainage basin of the Delaware River Valley;

tidal marsh, thirty miles from Philadelphia. Tracing the shore is the line from him to her.

Her right frontal lobe had been flooded with blood from a burst vein. The neurologist showed the brain scan to my brother and me. "This is the pool of blood," he said, circling with his finger a gray space with a crooked border that spread across the screen—a lake overflowing its banks, "as when emotion too far exceeds its cause," Elizabeth Bishop says.

A map of my mother's saturated brain, and me driving her car across it, to Scott, to her. No, not that. What picture would convey the dread and romance of whatever was about to be gone, the life of the beloved whom you manufacture and pursue in order to believe in the possibility that you were loved, or might have been loved, or could be loved if only your timing were better, or you were better?

A brain scan, a map, darkened pools on a glowing screen. My mother's body in a hospital bed, diapered, swaddled in a blue-flecked white gown, laid on white sheets. Scott's body in need of drugs to keep him alive, to keep his body from eating itself alive. Scott in the north of Pennsylvania, my mother in the south, me in a toy car on a torn map of cheap thin paper like the kind you get in roadside filling stations from the 1960s, with the seams split and the colors faded green and blue and white.

If I lose Scott, I thought, I will never be able to think of Allentown again without feeling absurd pain. That'll be it for the Delaware Water Gap!

I was prepared to lose my mother. The surprise was not losing her.

I held Scott for a few hours. Then I got in my mother's car and drove as fast as I could to her kitchen, in time to make omelets for her and Joy. "If you don't eat more," I told my mother, "they're sending you back to the hospital." She said, "I'd rather go to Trenton than that hospital."

"Trenton's right over there," I say, pointing to Jersey. "The car's outside. Are you going to eat?"

"I am going to drive into the Delaware River and die with my dog," she says, "before I ever go back to the hospital."

"You can't drive," I tell her. "You're not allowed to drive."

"I will drive my car."

"I won't let you drive."

"Then you can," she says. "You will drive."

"And we'll both drown."

"And so will the dog."

"You want all of us to drown?"

"I don't care who drowns," she says. "As long as I do."

Your Nostalgia Is Killing Me

Scott was going to run out of his HIV medication in twenty-eight days. That's what he told me. We were in his house in the woods. It was a two-story white frame house off a road that followed the course of a stream. The owner had split the building into three apartments, and Scott had the ground floor. Temporary digs. He had Cancer rising. Astrologically. Hermit crab. He liked to crawl into other people's shells and hide there. From late fall until early spring, I was driving every week or so to Pennsylvania, to some house way back in the woods where Scott lived for now.

I don't think he liked me. Does that sound abject? I'm trying to stick to the facts. He kept his distance. When I was first getting to know him, face-to-face, after he drove across the country from California to start over on the East Coast, he came down to New York a few times, August to October, and we sat outside in small parks in the West Village drinking coffee from deli cups. Then I started going up there to see him in the Pennsylvania woods. I don't like woods, but that's where he was. I found him in four different houses, on the banks of two rivers and a stream: a cabin on the Susquehanna River, two cabins near the Delaware River, and the ground-floor apartment in a house that backed up to a stream, part of a network of streams that slid along the blue shale of the Poconos to empty into the Delaware.

It was March now. We were in his white frame house, in the big front room that opened out from the kitchen. There were two other rooms—his office, where he wrote screenplays and the rants that he posted to Facebook and his blog; and his bedroom, where he slept on a mattress on the floor with the stray cats who found Scott the way he found me, by following an instinct for survival to open arms and a bowl of milk.

We were standing near the door in our winter coats and knit caps and work boots, two cisgender gay white men in their fifties dressed like dairy farmers as if we were regular guys with necessary lives and cattle out back.

I had just walked through the door, which I hadn't shut. We stood in the chill breeze, not speaking or making a move, as if we were waiting for someone to yell, "Scene!" before we stepped onstage. "Don't get ready," an acting teacher warned me once, in an acting class in the West Village, thirty years ago. It was his favorite phrase. You'd be about to start your scene, which you had carefully rehearsed, and he'd hiss, "Don't get ready." You were just supposed to walk out there and *be*.

Don't prepare to live, just live. It sounds like a Facebook meme. Scott was ready all the time—ready for this thing right now, for the road trip, change of plans, a film treatment someone said he should write, which he would sit down to write, and nearly finish, until something more exciting, beautiful but costly, better because more perilous, until something faster, more fun, a new guy who would not keep track of the past, showed up.

I was not that guy. The one who didn't keep track, or didn't mind what you lost or refused or forgot. Who didn't add things up. I might have seemed to be that guy at first. It was the worst thing about me. False advertising. Because I kept track of everything and reminded you in the morning: oh, by the way. Last night, last week, last June. You said this. You did that.

On the other hand, Scott would not risk his feelings, just yours. He was fearless about your feelings. As for his feelings, he was a commuter who had moved to the farthest outlying suburb in order to take forever to reach the center of town, which, after all, had no center.

We were finally learning these things about each other. That Scott would never appear. That I would never stop calling roll.

All I wanted was to be responsible for him. If only it had been up to me to mark him absent—me and nobody else, including himself.

We stood there, looking at each other. I reached out and put my hand around the back of his neck and pulled his face to mine, and then I grabbed his arms and wrapped them around my waist. "Hold on to me," I said. "That's why I'm here."

He was laughing, and he buried his face in my shoulder.

"I'm glad you're here," he said.

We were going to drive into the small town a mile down the road to get drugs. Not drugs, medications. He had run out of his antianxietals, accidentally or on purpose, I never figured out. I'm not sure he knew. Klonopin, which is for epilepsy, but also panic disorders. There were other meds. He had listed them all for me one morning when he showed me his pillbox. I had never seen so many different pharmaceuticals together in one container, and I'm a gay man from New York who has lived through nearly forty years of the global AIDS crisis.

Scott had—forgotten? neglected? refused?—to refill his psychotropic meds, and he had decided, when the pills were gone, to live without them. Drug holiday. For the past week, he had been in flight, in a rental car, moving fast through central Pennsylvania, as far as Harrisburg, "visiting old friends," he said, and withdrawing from antidepressants, cold turkey.

He posted to Facebook about driving his car into a ditch by the side of the road near Hershey, miles from home. His Facebook page was a chronicle of personal disasters with a fifteen-minute time delay. Sometimes he posted news of what went wrong before it really did, and he would have to hurt himself in order to prove his post right. Did he steer fast into a ditch because he'd said he had? It was during one of the recurring periods when we weren't speaking. I had stopped seeing him, or "liking" his Facebook posts, modern love. He asked me to stop, and I had stopped.

Yet here he was barreling into a ditch, and I read his post—it showed up in my Facebook newsfeed, copied to someone else's page—and I called him, and said, "Hershey? Are you covered in chocolate?" And he said, "Chocolate almond." And I said, "I'm coming to find you," and he said, "Really?" Relieved, not incredulous. We were laughing, but not joking. He was in trouble, and he sounded crushed and sad and uncertain.

Jesus, the scene in my head of Scott in peril. I said where would I find him, and he said I'll meet you at home, I'm driving home, and I said was his car even working, and he said it was working enough, and I said would he please drive carefully, and he said it would be okay.

I pictured his endangered body lying by the side of the road, and I was crying on the phone, which was not a manipulation, though he was always kinder when I cried. He liked to cry, he liked to watch people cry, and I am not a crier. I cry alone at war movies; that's it. But I cried once a week with Scott. "Will you please be okay," I said, "I want you to be okay," and he said, "I'll be okay," in a tone that meant he would forgive me for caring about him.

For now, he forgave me, and it was okay.

We went back out his front door, which he shut behind him but didn't lock, and we crossed the short span of gray porch to a path through the snow that led to the muddy, rutted drive where I had parked my car with the driver's side door swung wide open and the car beeping because I'd left the keys in the ignition.

"Park your car down the hill," he said. "We'll take mine."

Of course his car, even his crashed car. He did not like to sit in other people's cars, relinquish control. And his car was miraculously unwrecked. Had he invented the crash? It was not just unscathed, it was rented free because his truck was in the shop, and there were reasons why he had been given a free car for two weeks. Somebody had backed into his truck, and the insurance company—his or someone else's—had offered up a free rental, unlimited miles. It came the minute his antidepressants ran out. So he went on the road. Fated events? I could never follow the twists and turns of Scott's luck, which consisted of what could be salvaged unexpectedly from loss.

I'm not saying I'm not disturbed. I'm obviously disturbed. Scott and I had both been flung from a crash, and I was standing over our bodies on the pavement, outlining them with a piece of yellow chalk, while Scott picked through the wreckage, finding something newly useful that had been wrenched loose in the collision and carrying it away.

I parked my car in a small lot downhill from the house where Scott lived for now and got in beside him in his rented car, a little over a year since we'd met on a Facebook page for survivors of the AIDS crisis.

We had both lived in New York in the 1980s and nineties, and though we had never met back then, we had gone to the same protests, yards away from each other in chanting crowds, with hundreds, sometimes thousands of people who were fighting the lack of government response to AIDS, lack of medical care and research, lack of humane drug testing, lack of a cure, lack of shame among so many Americans who let their shunned children die alone on hospital gurneys in the hallways of AIDS wards. And now, in the past few years, the early history of AIDS activism was being "rediscovered"—documented, memorialized, curated, taught in schools, given a linear storyline, its "leaders" whitewashed and appointed in retrospect, its artifacts exhibited in museums, its actions and interventions dramatized and shown on TV. Its successes made to seem lasting and definitive. Its costly and continued failures overlooked.

We were statistics, objects of study, subjects of recent documentaries and nightly newscasts and "Style" section photo spreads, encased in Scott's car and headed for Rite Aid. The car was shiny and new, its dashboard glowing in the dark. Blankets covered the back seat for the cats. He had taken a few of them on his recent vexed trip to the interior.

They were feral cats, not cute and cuddly cats, and why did they not fight, scratch, and claw? The cats got along with each other; they were calm in Scott's arms.

Beck sang from the glowing dash. Depressed white boy music: let the banjo strumming in the background remind you with false nostalgia of being the center of the world. Scott and I had been raised to occupy the center, but we were queer, and the feeling of being exiled, denied access to power we were promised but knew we hadn't earned, had made us touchy and self-dramatizing.

Scott by the side of the road. His car in a ditch. Cats flying around his head, a painting by Salvador Dali. Cats flung in the air, frozen in time and space, legs and tails outstretched. Scott a surrealist portrait, beautiful and bloodied.

The road from his house to the center of town cut a square angle to the shopping street—not the historical street with pretty red brick federal houses, but a street lined with gas stations and convenience stores, running to the state highway. The drugstore was past the liquor store. We parked and went through the store to the pharmacy counter in back.

The emptiness of a chain store outlet in a small town past dark. Fluorescent light shining off linoleum tiles. Rows of products on the shelves. Our stillness as we stood at the pharmacy counter. I stepped back, pointedly not watching, as if to create the illusion of privacy around Scott. I wanted to stage manage his safety.

He had called ahead to order his Klonopin. The scrip was ready for him, in a white bag. "That's it, we're good," I said, but he said, "Wait," and he leaned on the counter and asked in a different voice for his regular refill of HIV meds.

He hadn't yet told me—Facebook—anyone—that they were running out.

Then the woman behind the counter dropped her voice and said that his Medicare had been canceled last week, and he would have to pay full price not just for the Klonopin, but also the Stribild, the AIDS drug, which he usually bought in a three-month supply that cost three hundred dollars, but that, without insurance, she was sorry, would cost twenty-seven-hundred dollars.

Scott stepped away from the counter. He said he knew that was going to happen. He was holding the bag with the plastic container of Klonopin inside. It made a rattling sound. The paper crinkled. "Shit, my insurance," he said. He said, "I shouldn't have left California. I shouldn't have left," he said. "I knew this would happen. Shit."

We stood under a bright light, and Scott was crying, and I rubbed his shoulders and said it would be okay. I said, "I'm sorry," and, "It'll be okay." He said again he knew this would happen. I didn't know how to help him. I never know. I've watched friends die, and I have never been any help except to hold you and say, "I'm sorry."

A long time later, he told me that everything I did or didn't do gave him pain.

"You're too intense," he said.

We got back in his car. He had forgotten to bring his wallet. He didn't even have the cash in his pocket to pay for what he could afford. Of course, he didn't have credit cards. Neither did I. We were the only two gay men in North America who didn't. I like men whose lives are even more slipshod than mine. We left the bag of Klonopin on the counter, went back to his house, and got the wallet. We went back to the drugstore, with the wallet, and paid for the Klonopin, and then we got in his car and went back to his house. That was when he said he had enough Stribild to last twenty-eight days. Stribild was a combination drug, one pill a day containing the necessary meds—two nucleoside reverse transcriptase inhibitors and a protease inhibitor—to block the replication of HIV in his bloodstream and keep his viral load undetectable and his body safe.

We were in his kitchen. He was making tea. Neither one of us had twenty-seven-hundred dollars, right then, though I had a steady income and a permanent job, which Scott did not. There were cats around our feet and Scott put milk down for the cats and I was backed against the refrigerator. Why am I always backed against someone's refrigerator door in a crisis? The worst moments of my life played out against the sound of that aluminum thrum.

If you went off your AIDS meds in the twenty-first century, you'd die like it was 1989. And people went off their meds, and they died. People who were lucky enough to get AIDS meds nonetheless sometimes stopped taking them. Because they were depressed. Because they were isolated and alone. Because they were bored, because they were broke, because they hadn't planned to still be here by now.

I knew that if Scott were left to himself, he would not get more HIV meds between now and the end of twenty-eight days. He would let his meds run out, gather his cats around him, and wait however long it took, six months, maybe a year, to die. And post to Facebook about it.

We stood in his kitchen with the refrigerator's drone, drinking tea and feeding wounded cats, and counting out the pills left in Scott's multicolored plastic pillbox with its compartments: green and blue and red snap-shut lids labeled with days of the week. "I'll move to New York," he said. "Or just pretend I moved there. I'll call about the insurance tomorrow. It's so much better in New York. Who should I call? Is there, like, a Big Insurance Switchboard?" We made a list of people and places he would call. "I'll establish residency in New York. I don't have to move there. I'll stay in Pennsylvania; New York will pay for things. The promised land."

He had a soft voice, with a tremor in the background like something wrong with your car. Something negligible that anyone could fix, any mechanic, just not you.

"Listen, Scott," I said. "Can you buy a month's supply of Stribild? Not you, I mean, but anyone. Does it only come in, like, a jumbo box? Like you get at Costco? Three-months' supply?"

"You can get a month's worth, yeah."

"So, I have enough cash for a month. All right? In my checking account. How much is a month?"

"Forget it."

"Just listen."

"I'm not taking your money. I can't pay you back."

"I said listen. I don't want it back. What's it cost for a month? Like, eight hundred dollars, or—"

"A little more than that."

"I'm giving you eight hundred dollars. That's what I have. I have about a thousand, actually, but the ATM's got a limit. Daily limit. So I can give you eight hundred. Right now, tonight. Okay? I'm not asking. It's not your choice."

"No."

"That's not the right answer."

"No, I can't."

"Doesn't matter if you can't. It's what you'll do."

"How would I pay you back?"

"You wouldn't."

"I can't pay you back."

"I don't want you to pay me back. It's a gift. There's an ATM at the drugstore. I'll get the cash, and they *have* the pills already, right?"

"A three months' supply."

"So they'll pour you out a month's worth. One month. Thirty days. Add that to the pills you've already got, it'll give you two months to figure out what to do. Get your insurance in shape. Move to Peekskill. Whatever. Because, otherwise, you're going to be stressed out every one of those twenty-eight days."

"Anyway, it's closed by now. The pharmacy counter is closed."

"Just the counter, not the store. I'll give you the money tonight, and you can go back tomorrow without me. "

"And tomorrow it'll be twenty-seven days."

"See? Not that you're counting. Scott. I'm not giving you a choice."

"I'll pay you back."

"You're never paying me back. Forget that. I don't care. I have the money, you don't. So it's yours. The money doesn't matter. You know, 'From each according to his ability, to each according to his—'"

"My little communist."

"Just, you should be okay. Say yes."

He didn't exactly say yes.

We drove to the drugstore again, the third time that night, and I pulled eight hundred bucks in big bills from an ATM by the lipstick display. Then I jumped in Scott's car, shotgun, and we made for the woods, dust-bowl bank robbers on the lam from the law in 1932. I offered to marry him, but he was already married, in California, to a man. They had gotten hitched in the brief pause between California's granting queers the right to marry and then taking it away.

If he couldn't get an address in New York by the end of the month, he would use the money and buy more pills. Those were his conditions for accepting the cash. "Hide the money, don't tell me where it is until I need it, which I won't," he said, and I stuffed the loot in a white envelope and stashed it in the way back of a kitchen drawer, behind the steak knives, and we were boyfriends again. Conditional boyfriends. Adulterers. Health care bandits. Bonnie and Clyde.

They didn't have sex either.

* * *

I never said a thing to anyone about Scott or my trips to Scott. Because he was married? The marriage was over, he said. He had come east because it was over. I didn't even mention him on Facebook. And I put *everything* on Facebook. Everything but Scott. No road-trip selfies, no cute shots of us in the woods. Was I ashamed? Because we were sleeping together but not having sex? We watched Barbara Stanwyck movies instead, in bed with the cats. Then he talked and talked, and cried in my arms, and fell asleep. Is that not sex?

Our relationship was a secret, probably also from him.

Yet after Scott's road trip to a Hershey ditch, we spent nearly every weekend together, from Ash Wednesday to Mother's Day.

My trips to Scott in darkness, or the plain light of day. Wherever he was. Everything I saw on the way to Scott, ordinary or sublime— Dairy Queens, mountaintops—was Scott, the roads and bridges, toll booths, farmhouses, sudden democratic vistas, dun flat four-way country intersections after dark in the far north of Jersey. Who knew there was so much of Jersey between Secaucus and Suffern? The everyday world that led to Scott was infused with deep feeling, like the picture of a refrigerator that Virginia Woolf's little James Ramsay endows with "heavenly bliss" when he hears his mom say maybe they will swing by the lighthouse tomorrow. I was intoxicated by Scott, as well as the trips to Scott. Woolf would say I was one of those who paint the world with their desire so that everything you see and hear and touch is part of what you anticipate and love.

I leaned forward in my seat and craned my neck as if it were not Scott but meaning I was promised. Family, finally. Connection. Speeding out of the city, down strange streets, I had Google maps and my will to get there. Which to my surprise, I did, without needing to back up, or turn around, or stop at a Mobil Mart in Pompton Lakes and ask the guy behind the plexiglass where I was. By the time I reached Scott, my neck was stiff and my muscles sore and I was tense and tired and someone else. I had been erased by dislocation and the need to belong, my car a rescue craft, the *Rachel* come round to unshipwreck Ishmael at the end of *Moby Dick*.

One cold weekend in late March, headed north through Pennsylvania because Scott had gotten a paid house-sitting gig up near the southern border of New York, I drove back and forth across the Susquehanna River on a two-lane road that swooped and climbed and dove down and stuck me behind a line of cars until it widened in a passing lane, the sky thick with snow that spun at me as if aimed. Reaching Scott was as mesmerizing as a scene from Edgar Allan Poe where the self slips through the known world at the South Pole.

A transcendental errand into the wilderness. At the end of the road was Scott in a warm cabin with a wood-burning stove. The room was smoky; the stove was not quite working. Scott was a step below me, our chins made level by the raised landing where I stood with my arms out halfway between relief and entreaty. He hugged me, laughed and kissed me, and said, "My boyfriend, in from the cold."

It could have been true. I had come all this way and been rewritten by time and distance, and I was not me, but a possible boyfriend pressed to a man's chest. A familiar man I hardly knew.

And all the while, there was cash in a drawer and a calendar whose sheets ripped off and blew past like in a 1930s black-and-white film montage. Twenty-five days, twenty-one, nineteen . . .

We had two plans: A and B. Plan A was he would get a legal address in New York, then insurance, then drugs. Plan B was when the drugs were about to run out, I would call him on the phone and say, "Plan B," and tell him where the money was, and he would find it, and take it to the drugstore, and spend it on a month's supply of Stribild. Even if his New York address and/or his new insurance were just days away.

"Or even hours," he said.

"Please don't make me wait until you're hours away from running out of drugs."

"Make who wait? Make *you* wait?"

"That's not what I mean. You know what I mean."

"Do you get a Boy Scout merit badge for saving me? I'm a knot you're learning to tie?"

"*Untie.* Scott. Do you remember AIDS in 1985? When you'd die from viruses that *birds* got? Aviary bugs are sanding down the walls of your intestines, you've got diarrhea, your body's eating itself because it can't digest anything else, and you're stunned and diapered and covered in lesions and going blind and insane?"

He was quiet. "Anyway," I said. "Do you think you're *worth* a merit badge?" I was kidding. I think he knew. "A merit badge is like, building a temporary shelter in the Maine woods out of found objects and a torn shirt."

He was laughing. It would be okay. Most of the time, we laughed, on the phone, on FaceTime, in real time in the actual world, meeting wherever he materialized, however briefly, in the woods, in the city, in Washington Square Park, where he crossed his arms over his chest and shivered slightly in a thin sweater, none of his clothes protective or warm or really his size. He dressed as if to say that the body he had, and was, had just removed itself from your gaze or grasp. I loved him for what he couldn't do: reach out, call back, let me . . .

He'd say I'm describing myself. He was clever at that, deflecting complaint.

Once when I shot him a hurt email at two in the morning, he sent it back annotated and twice as long, going through my message point by point and refuting me like a lawyer at a small-town assembly meeting fighting the construction of a new jail. He turned around each of my grievances and showed how they really applied, not to him, but me.

"Never contact me again," he said, in closing.

Days later, after I was banished, it was my birthday, and he called all cheery and invited me up to a different house in another part of the woods. We were putative boyfriends again, weekend guests of a rich guy he met on Facebook, at a landmarked house in a town laid out in Quaker orderliness on an escarpment above the Delaware River. Scott's new friend wore a white chef's hat without irony, and he made sorrel soup and *boeuf en daube*, and for dessert, we ate hash brownies, in a dining room hung with silkscreens from Warhol's "Death and Disaster" series—crashed cars, electric chairs; and later, in a third-floor bedroom, Scott took off all his clothes for the first time in front of me, in the dark, and we lay naked holding each other.

"Happy birthday," he said. And with his head on my chest, he cried and said he hated having and being a body. There were men who had abused him, long ago. I offered to kill them. I meant it. He told me stories of abuse that I won't repeat because this is violation enough. He said he felt small, though he was not. He felt his body was perilously small, and he was ashamed of the attention he got. Ashamed and dependent upon. Attention from everyone—straight women, gay men, everybody he had ever loved, the men who exploited him. His family. Himself. God, probably. Representatives of God.

I don't want to exploit him or diminish him.

His arms, though.

Jesus Christ.

He had a big relaxed body that he seemed to have fought for. A gym body he was starting to neglect. I like what's almost over. If you stood with him watching a river flow downstream after a storm, in the minute after the storm passed, a bad storm, so that the air was heavy with the feeling of returning to calm, a little too late—he was like that.

He told me he hated sex, but he was known for posting rants to his blog and Facebook page about how much he missed it. How a generation of gay men had been robbed, by AIDS, of sex. How older gay men with HIV were still being robbed. He wanted sex back. He had left California and come home to the East Coast to recover sex.

And to recover from sex, I found out.

I was his recovery from sex.

It was rehab, not an affair. Though it had the elements of an affair—secrecy, passionate declarations, an irresistible sense of doom.

He had been used by men and later rejected by men because he had HIV. We were going to figure out how to be intimate in an epidemic if the epidemic was not HIV but masculinity in America. We would help each other to be different men.

It was a long winter and late spring, the whiteness of ground and sky a background to our collision. Not Robert Frost death-white, but the grayish-white of snow pocked with gravel and roadkill through northeastern Pennsylvania. I won't get metaphorical about what we couldn't do. Yet it seems to me still that we loved each other, the way people usually love, happily, angrily, inconsistently, well enough, wanting the best for each other. Sometimes not wanting the best.

* * *

Three days before his meds ran out, he called me at school. I was teaching a course in AIDS Literature at a service college in Flushing, and I was showing my students a video animation about how the HIV virus replicates itself and wrecks your immune system. The green tennis ball of HIV, covered in yellow suction cups, was gaining on a fluffy white T-helper cell when my phone lit up with Scott's number.

I paused the AIDS video and excused myself and stepped into the hall.

"Plan B?" I said. "Finally?"

It was April. The original twenty-eight days had passed, but Scott had kept adding extensions, a day, a day, a day—finding pills that had fallen behind the cushions of his couch, or rolled under his refrigerator, or dropped into the wrong compartment of his pillbox. And he had lately rationed himself to a pill every other day, despite my pleading. No worries, he said. The paperwork for his New York address was always just about to go through. He had a cousin in Troy who was ready to claim, before the law, that Scott lived with him. A Trojan! Soon, Scott would have a warrior's address.

"I got it," he said. He didn't sound relieved. "The address."

"You got the—?"

"Day before yesterday."

"You were going to tell me?"

"It's on Facebook. I posted it to—"

"Scott. Should you be telling *Facebook*—"

"I'm legally a New Yorker. And I don't have to live there. I can stay here, and get my drugs there."

"Okay. Well. Okay. That's—"

"And I saw a doctor yesterday—"

"—great. That's great. And—?"

"—in Albany. A doctor and a psychiatrist and someone from social services, and—"

"—a doctor and shrink and a social worker. And?"

"They're going to get me the meds. I jumped through all their hoops. The insurance went through. I can get the prescriptions in two more weeks. They're basically free."

"You can get the—Scott, that's fantastic. That's—"

"Doesn't matter," Scott said. "I don't want them. The drugs. Fuck them. I have two pills left, but I don't care. I'm stopping my meds."

"You have two more pills. Perfect. Meanwhile, Plan B will tide you over. And then in two weeks—"

"I don't care. It's too late. I'm sick of this. It's humiliating. All those shrinks and social workers. I had to prove to them how fucked up I was. Fucked up and broke and alone—"

"You're not alone."

"—and if I'm broke and worthless and alone enough, they will let me have the drugs I need to survive."

I cracked open the classroom door, stuck my head in the room, and said, "Sorry." Held out my phone. "Family emergency," I said. Then I shut the door and walked to the far end of the hall. "Scott," I said. "What are you doing right now?"

"I haven't gotten out of bed."

"Okay. Good choice. Yay, you."

"It's 2:00 p.m."

"Best time of day to be in bed."

"I slept like fifteen hours. The cats woke me up. They're hungry."

"So that's a reason to get up. The shrink in Albany wants you alive so you can feed your cats. Why don't you get up and go to the kitchen and do that?"

"I'm not taking your money to the drugstore for two weeks of pills when I can get them free in New York."

"*In two weeks*, you can get them for free," I said. "Meanwhile. Meanwhile, you've got a bunch of angry cats."

"They're yowling."

"I hear that. So start with the cats. Okay? I'll stay on the phone. Can you just get up and—"

"Okay," he said. He was out of bed, he said, and it would be okay. He fed the cats. I stayed on the phone while he opened the fridge and got the food and filled the bowls. The cats were mewling. Then I talked him into taking his AIDS meds. One of his two remaining pills.

"I'll take the other one next week," he said. "That'll have to do me."

"Unless you get the money and call the drugstore and order a refill. Maybe they still have the bottle you didn't buy."

"I can wait two weeks."

"Those aren't the rules of the game."

"We're playing a game?"

"A game *show*," I said, "called *Stribild!* With antiretroviral drugs behind Door Number 3. I'm Joan Van Ark, your emcee, and this is the final round."

He said, "Joan Van Ark!"

It seemed possible that he believed me.

"Take your phone along, we'll walk around your house, and Joan will tell you how close you are to your cash."

"I'm headed for the office."

"Cold."

"Okay, I'm on my way to the front door. Under the rug?"

"Joan Van Ark is smarter than that."

"It's not under the rug."

"You knew it wouldn't be."

"Where else?"

"Why don't you go back to the kitchen? Imagine you were carving a steak."

"The knife drawer? Joan Van Ark, did you put the money in—?"

"Way in back."

"I'm reaching."

"All the way."

"Joan Van Ark has long arms."

"You found it? Behind the—"

"Thank you," he said.

"I left you a note," I said. "Under the knives."

"I see the note."

I was embarrassed. "You don't have to read it."

"I read it," he said. "Thank you."

"I just meant—"

"I know what you meant. I love you too," he said.

"Count the money."

"I'm counting it."

"You're *counting* it? You don't trust me?"

"You said to count it." We were both laughing. "Eight one-hundred dollar bills. Thank you. Okay. I'll do it. Plan B. I'll go to the drugstore in town and do it."

"Text me a photo of the Stribild when you have it. All right? I want you to text me a photo. A picture of the bottle of Stribild."

"That's what I'll do. Thanks, Joan."

An hour later, he FaceTimed me. I was in my office at school. He was up in the woods behind his house, with, on his shoulder, his toughest meanest cat, the one who thought he was a dog, who would follow Scott on walks and bring dead mice to his bed. His name was Fritz. Fritz the Cat. I think Scott was staying alive for Fritz. Certainly not for me. Fritz was standing, not sitting, on Scott's right shoulder, like a parrot. Pirate Scott. I almost called him "Matey." But he had been letting his beard grow, and he looked like an Old Testament prophet in a lithograph by William Blake.

"You won't believe this," he said.

"Do you have the Stribild? I didn't get a text."

"You won't believe me when I tell you what happened. My luck is so weird."

"I know about your luck. Where's the Stribild?"

"I was standing," he said, "in the drugstore here in town. I was holding the bottle in my hand. They still had the refill from last time. The lady was nice about it. She poured me out enough for a month. I was just about to give them your money, and—"

"It's your money."

"Thank you for that. I can't thank you enough. Just listen to my luck, though. I was reaching for the money, about to hand it over, and I got a call. On my phone. From the pharmacy in New York. They have the drugs. Right now. I don't have to wait for two weeks. I can go to a place in Albany and pick up my scrips. I was about to give them your money."

"Scott, it's your money."

"They called in exactly that minute."

"So, now you have the drugs."

"I'm going to get them. Right now. It'll take an hour to get there."

"So you don't have the drugs."

"I'm on my way there. And I won't need your money. I'll text you when I get there. Promise. Thank you so much for your help. I would not have gotten up this morning if Joan Van Ark hadn't talked me into it. I was going to lie there and just wait for everything to end. You really, that was so, it was just, you knew just what to say."

"You'll text me a photo of the bottle?"

"I can't believe my luck."

"I love you," I said.

"I love you too," he said. "I'll text you."

Then he hung up, and I didn't hear from him for two weeks.

* * *

I fucked a guy last Thursday without a condom. Some guy. I didn't come inside him. My secret: I'm a top. It was the end of July. We were in downtown Philly, in a jerk-off parlor. I made five indifferent thrusts and stopped. How do you thrust indifferently? I found a way. Ten minutes in a dark basement. I don't have HIV. He said he didn't have HIV. People say that. His name was Ernie. I asked him twice, he gave the same name twice, and he gave me his number. I haven't called him.

Afterward, I went outside and smoked a cigarette. I haven't spoken to Scott in three months. Cigarettes are my transitional object. They don't work. I wasn't smoking when I was with Scott. I don't smoke. I got back to New York and went to a clinic and had my blood drawn by a counselor named Melody, who was sweet; and then a doctor named Don told me there was a 1 in 1,500 chance of my contracting HIV as a top without a condom, but if the guy had other STIs, the odds got worse. They ended up like 1 in 50. Don prescribed a twenty-eight-day regimen of PEP, HIV postexposure prophylaxis, Truvada, and Isentress, more transitional objects.

Eight hundred bucks for a month's worth.

Fortunately, I have decent insurance. New York State.

So I'm writing this on PEP, which makes me dizzy and vague. Factor that in.

* * *

He spent the money, of course. I still don't know on what.

Anyway, it was no longer in the drawer. The last time I saw him, I checked. Early in the morning, alone in the kitchen, with the cats.

Those early mornings leaving Scott's house. Weekday mornings. It was two hours back to Brooklyn from Scott's place, wherever he was. If I left too late, I hit the worst of rush-hour traffic. So I was awake even earlier than Scott, who kept farmers' hours, asleep by eight and up at four, not because he had to be in the dairy barn birthing calves, but because he was expected online. His blog rants and Facebook posts were some people's *Good Morning America.*

I'd wake at 3:30 a.m., slip out of bed, get dressed, and gather my stuff in the dark. Toothbrush and dental floss. Phone charger, power cord, cell phone, laptop: twenty-first century overnight kit. Shadowy light of the moon on the floor. Cats awake and brushing my legs hypocritically, like they cared about me, though what they wanted was breakfast, hours too soon. Sometimes I snuck them leftovers, swore them to secrecy. Sometimes I washed Scott's dishes, dried and stacked them, wrote a sappy note to stick under a refrigerator magnet.

Sometimes Scott got up and made coffee, and I took the mug and sipped it, not talking. We didn't speak. Two compulsive talkers, it was the only time we were silent, not explaining ourselves to each other—or rather, not explaining Scott, who was the subject of our relationship. Then, dressed and packed with my knapsack over my shoulder, in my coat and scarf and knit cap, I had the luxury of contrast in hugging him in his long johns and sweatshirt, Scott still half-sleeping while I was halfway out the door and headed into the day, not yet day.

The last time I saw him, it was May, and I took a commuter train up to a country station in a town on the border where New York, New Jersey, and Pennsylvania scrunch together and just touch. I don't know why I didn't have my car. I had gotten a good parking spot in Brooklyn and didn't want to move. Maybe that. He met me at the train, in his truck. We kissed, and he drove me up to the top of a hill overlooking the town. Scenic view. It was called Point Peter. Someone else named it, not me. The ground was doing what Thoreau sees in early spring,

thawed earth flowing downhill into sandy heaps like "lobed and im-
bricated thalluses of lichens."

Below us was the Delaware River town where Stephen Crane had
interviewed Civil War veterans in order to write *The Red Badge of
Courage.* We held hands above the convergence of the Delaware and
Neversink Rivers, looking down at the meth-lab town and talking
about buying a house. We figured out our finances, who could pay
what, like communists, from each, to each. Scott's disability payments.
My teacher's salary. He'd write screenplays, and I'd commute to work.

I didn't ask about the drugs. When or where he had finally gotten
them. I assumed at least that he *had* gotten them, and was taking them.

The next day, early morning, I snuck a look in the steak knife
drawer. Maybe he had put the cash back there for an emergency. It
was his money. I wanted him to have it. I knew it wouldn't be there,
and it wasn't. Then he was awake and making coffee, and he drove me
to the train.

That was the last time I saw him.

He was sleeping with a twenty-two-year-old kid who lived on
Eastern Parkway in Brooklyn, not far from my apartment. Someone I
had once bought a cheeseburger after a Queer Nation rally protesting
anti-gay laws in Vladimir Putin's Russia.

On the way home, on the commuter train, speeding through the
Jersey woods, I checked Facebook and saw that Scott had posted a
selfie with the kid. He was kissing him. The selfie had been posted
that morning—while I was snooping in his kitchen drawer. "I love this
man," the caption said.

"It is not good that man should be alone," Yahweh says, watching
Adam stagger around the Garden, searching for love, asking everything he saw, "Are you my angel?" Which of the beasts that slid upon
the earth, which that walked on four good legs, was his angel? Which
that swam in the sea? Was it the fish? No. Was it the duck? No. The
pomegranate? God intervened. "I will make him an helpmeet for him."

Was I his helpmeet? Was he mine?

The first time I saw him in the material world, in the West Village, after weeks of talking online, he lumbered towards me, saying, "Friend! Friend!" Boris Karloff as Frankenstein's monster with his legs stiff and arms outstretched to cradle the girl he was about to drown.

Only I was worthless! No one else. Was I competitive even about abjection? Middle-class white guy in America, I had lost status because I was a fag, and how would I regain my spot at the center, as essential? Like this:

Only I could save you.

I thought I saw him on the street just now. I'm in Fishtown. Philadelphia. Why would he be in Philly? Why would I? At a hipster café called the Rocket Cat. The guy I saw through the café window wasn't dressed like Scott: straw hat, orange slacks, golfing shirt. Not Scott. I lost sight of him; then I ran outside to look for Scott's truck. I wasn't sure I would recognize it. Did it still have California plates? I had given Scott money, a few hundred bucks, to fix its bumper or its taillight or something.

The agony of that age, twenty-five years ago. The crisis we lived through, at the same time, in the same city. Shit smears on white sheets, bones in sight under skin. The litany of weird diseases only birds got. The trauma of that time.

When we met online, it was as if we had always known each other because the trauma we lived through had defined us, equally; submerged us. Not submerged like Marcel Proust in his bed, remembering every room where he ever slept, warm beneath his covers, pillows over his head for protection from his dreams. No. Submerged like someone's got you by the neck at the Jersey shore and is holding you under the waves, wave after wave, and you're terrified and twelve, and where are your parents? The man who holds you is not a stranger. He's someone you know. And he's dipping the receptacle of your face again and again in the waves, filling your mouth with sand and salt water, and you understand that you're a container. An object into which someone spills his rage, then empties you out so you're ready for more.

I know I'm intense.

I know he's alive because of me. I'm sure of that. That last time I saw him, he was alive because of me. I also know he would have lived without me, and sooner or later, he'll die without me.

We had fought to stay alive, and now we were alive.

We had fought to keep each other alive, and here we were.

I'm not saying he was worth it.

The insulated one-cup coffee thermos he gave me filled with hot coffee is still in the back of my car, empty and rolling around.

Imitation of Life

*I really wanted to come off a lot more, uh, a lot more brutal—
simply, as I said before, just simply to show that I was going on,
and someday I was gonna be bruised or battered enough to be
able to understand some other way of life.*
      —Lance Loud
        interviewed by Dick Cavett, 1973

It Gets Worse

It's 1970. September, early morning, rural northwestern New Jersey. Lebanon Township Elementary School, Kindergarten through eighth grade, at the head of Bunnvale Road, an old coach road in a series of swoops that go flat for horse teams to catch their breath before climbing the next steep hill. Upward-winding rollercoaster road. The school building, one story, red with white trim, laid along the road and facing cornfields, is long and narrow and swollen at both ends in blocky extrusions: cafeteria, gymnasium. Barbell-shaped, dumbbell building. Kindergarten classrooms near the cafeteria at the bottom, from which children, like horses, climb, grade by grade, to the eighth-grade classrooms up against the gym.

When you reach eighth grade, you graduate to the big county high school ten miles away.

I'm in sixth grade, with the big kids. Everyone from fourth grade down is little kids, with fourth-grade classrooms halfway, dividing stations.

A half hour before the morning bell, yellow school buses arrive in a fleet as if synchronized and park on black asphalt before the building in single-line formation, disgorging kids whose heads and arms are reflected in the classroom windows.

White kids, Catholic and Protestant, German and Irish and Dutch and Scotch-Irish, two Jewish families, one black family, a few Polish and Italian kids, a girl whose mom is French, one whose mom is Japanese. A few kids whose dads commute to Rahway or Scotch Plains.

Mostly farm kids, the children of chicken farmers, dairy farmers, or their dads drive trucks, and their moms work in the school cafeteria. Or they own junkyards, or coach boys' intramural basketball, or teach the fourth grade.

Special Needs kids who are not getting their needs met will spend high school in Special Ed. Some really poor kids. Two sisters in hand-me-down housedresses who miss school for months. Mocked and ignored by their classmates, including me. Kids who have been held back a year or two and are always awkwardly bigger and older. Kids who didn't get the right health care young enough and are living with the consequences.

I'm weird. My father works sixty miles away in Manhattan, and my mother rides her retired racehorse bareback in sneakers with a rope for a bridle in the big mown field behind the school. She does not bake pies. She does not mentor Girl Scouts. She takes her horse commando coursing in the woods.

Foothills of the Jersey Highlands. Low mean hills, rocky deposits. Coach roads, back roads, river roads of rutted dirt, icy in winter, washed out in spring, narrow hill roads paved with gravel and tar. Bunnvale Road is anchored by two general stores. Not convenience stores, not 7-11s; there is no such thing. Wooden sagging nineteenth-century corner stores. At the bottom of the road, across County Highway 513, is the Bunnvale Store. At the top of the hill, where Bunnvale Road crosses Hill Road and turns into Woodglen Road, is the Woodglen Store.

Roads and stores and schools named by imagist poets: the road that goes to Bunnvale is the Bunnvale Road. The road that goes through a woody glen is the Woodglen Road. The hilltop school laid naked to the elements is the Elementary School. Whatever it seems, it is, and that's also its name.

Literal, ruined landscape. Robert Frost's poems about stone foundations of missing houses, "only a belilaced cellar hole closing like a dent in dough." Jersey as exhausted New Hampshire. "House no more a house, farm no more a farm." Up-thrusting sawtooth solitary stone walls of crumbling churches. A burned-down house and its outbuildings, horse barns and hay barns, charred, vacant, filled with dog turds and trash from the 1950s. Clogged ponds in cement beds. Railroad tracks that run to the Musconetcong River but don't cross it, stone pylons for their vanished trestles looming over the river bank. Abandoned cars in open fields, '57 Chevys with shattered windshields and sprung rotting seats. Dead bodies of gutted deer left behind by hunters, poachers. Private family cemeteries up in the woods, overgrown with weeds and trees, big rocks for headstones. Rock walls lining fields that have long since returned to forest, dogwood, skunk cabbage, walking fern, shadbush, pitcher plants that drown bugs, rain-soaked mossy logs, poison ivy, poison oak.

American pastoral.

Converted barns and makeshift summer homes. Adirondack cabins lacking heat and plumbing. New five-and-dime development houses bent over the crest of a hill, Boulder Field. Families have been living for one-hundred-fifty years in log cabins and tarpaper shacks along the South Branch of the Raritan River. Also exiles from New York, failed actors, magazine illustrators, in summer cottages their parents bought for a nickel during the Depression. And in Changewater, down along the Musconetcong River, a commune where Dave Dellinger of the Chicago Seven founded *Liberation* magazine in 1956 with Bayard Rustin and A. J. Muste.

The point of the place being that it's somewhere you can print an anarchist newspaper in the Eisenhower era and nobody, including your neighbors, will notice.

Rural American privacy.

* * *

It's 7:45 a.m. I'm outside behind the school building with the big kids, including all fifty members of the sixth-grade class, waiting for the bell to ring and the day to start. It's Election Day. I'm running for sixth-grade class president, and my pants are too short. "Clamdiggers." I'm white, blond, blue-eyed, eleven years old. My hair, in a crew cut, stands up in a cowlick in front.

I was president of the fourth grade, my peak. Downhill since. None of the other boys are as smart as the girls, none of them as bad at sports.

We're at the big double doors by the gym, in a patch of ground covered with small round gray rocks that make a crunching sound. The school faces the road, but we're in back.

Behind us, a field ending in a line of pine trees. Down below us, near the entrance for the little kids, are a slide and a couple of swings.

We're on the flat top of a bare hill.

Kids are wearing light fall jackets. Cool kids carry their lunches in paper sacks. The rest of us still have our third-grade lunch pails, decorated with scenes from Saturday morning cartoons, *Underdog*, *Fireball XL5*.

The air smells like library paste and pencil shavings, and the bubble-gum-flavored toothpaste scent of my classmates.

The Beatles are playing on somebody's transistor radio. Paul McCartney wants me back where I belong.

I wrote a speech to read at our election rally. It's folded in my hand. I'm nervous and distracted, and I don't notice that a circle is forming around me until somebody calls my name.

"Sally," he says. "Sally," he says again, and I ignore it. I'm not big enough or strong enough to hit anybody, and anyway, I'm antiwar. Nonviolent resistance! "When an angry dog goes after you," my mother says, "don't react." And I know the guy. He hits home runs, and I let him cheat off my tests in English class.

Then he says, "Sally Fay." A twist. "Sally *Fay*," he says again, pleased with himself, and he pushes me.

I'm waiting for it to turn into a joke. It doesn't. The next time he says it, somebody joins in. Then someone else. It's a chant. "Sally Fay. Sally Fay." That's when the circle closes around me. It happens fast. Everyone in the sixth grade is pushing me. Anyway, all the boys. Bumper pool, and I'm the ball. I bounce off different parts of the circle while they call me "Sally Fay," like we're drag queens instead of eleven-year-olds. They try more new names. Maybe the first time any of us have heard them or said them. Grace notes over the melody line: "Faggot." "Homo." "Gay Faggot." "Queer."

My last name rhymes with "queer." What choice do they have? Anyway, what's in a name?

Wyrd is Old English for "destiny" or "fate"; and *faie* is Middle English for "fairy," or "fay" or "fey," from the Old English *faege*, meaning "fated to die soon." A "faggot" is a bundle of sticks thrown on a pyre to burn witches, and "faggoting" is a decorator's term for something you do with lace. "Queer" is Germanic, from the root *thwerh-*, meaning "twisted," and the Old Norse *thverr*, which means "to thwart."

So I'm twisted, thwarted and thwarting, fairy-like but fateful, not just silly but lethal, not just deadly but fated to die, kindling for fire, powerful and burning, but also inconsequential, dainty as threads pulled tight around delicate lace. And I'm the star. That's what's confusing. Trapped in their circle, surrounded and alone, I'm rejected and central, and here is the beginning of my lifelong inability to tell the difference between attention and pain.

Dodgeball. Two teams in Boys' Gym throw a hard brown rubber ball back and forth. Get hit, and you're out. Or catch the ball someone throws, and they're out. Play until the last two boys face off. The tough, mean, athletic boys are the ones who catch the ball and throw it back. They throw hard, and the ball stings thighs and leaves welts.

I hide in back and dart around, which protects me, not forever, because I end up the last kid on my side, facing a boy with a throwing arm and dead aim.

"Get the queer," my classmates yell as he winds up for the throw.

✳ ✳ ✳

My mother macramés a scarf. Red, gray, wool, with fringe. Flung around my neck and trailing behind me like Mick Jagger at Altamont singing "Gimmer Shelter." In the hallway, between classes, my friends grab the scarf, pull it tight around my neck, choke and kick me, and call me a fag.

✳ ✳ ✳

Eighth-grade music class. We're about to sing "Home on the Range." Our music teacher, Mrs. Westerly, buxom and corseted like a Wagnerian soprano, hands out lyrics on mimeographed sheets. Then she puts a sing-along record on the phonograph. She runs her finger over the needle with a scratching popping sound and drops the stylus in the groove. As she raises her hands to conduct, we sing. At the refrain, "Home, home on the range," my classmates turn to me and sing, in unison, "Ho-*mo* on the range."

✳ ✳ ✳

Bullying is typical, right? Universal?

"I got called a fag, and I'm *straight*. Get over it," a straight guy says.

"Every queer got called a fag in seventh grade. I'm over it," a gay guy says.

When I grew up, a faggot getting choked in a grade-school hallway wasn't typical.

Faggots were *unique*.

I was the only faggot I knew.

Were there other faggots?

I was looking for proof that there were other fags.

Paul Lynde?

My parents weren't faggots, my brother was not a faggot, none of my friends were faggots, there were no soap operas about bullied faggots. If only it had felt universal! But it felt particular, isolated, only. It felt queer: unlike. Local, personal. Alone. My shame and narcissism: it was painful, and it was all about me.

✻ ✻ ✻

High school, sophomore year. The new choir director is young and hip. We call him "Mr. O." In front of everyone, in the middle of class, autumn afternoon, he interrupts himself and says, out loud, to me, "You know, you walk like a girl."

Everyone laughs. I laugh.

He says, "No. Really. You do. Somebody get up and show him how he walks."

All my friends are in the room. Best friends. My brother, my brother's girlfriend. It's basically the drama club. Everybody here is probably a fag, though I'm the faggot of all fags.

A bunch of guys raise their hands. "Let me, let me do his walk."

Mr. O picks Mark. A greaser. I mock people too. I'm a vicious mocker. Mark's hair is big in front and slicked in a duck's ass in back. For Spring Concert last year, he wore a leisure suit and sang, flat, "Does Anybody Really Know What Time It Is?"

He's Andy Kaufman ahead of his time. If it were ten years later, he'd have a sitcom. But it's 1974 in Annandale, New Jersey, and he goes to the front of the choir room and walks back and forth, doing me, while my friends yell advice.

"Swish your hips."

"Dangle your wrists."

Mr. O isn't happy. "That's not it," he says. Mark sits down, and Mr. O takes over. "You're not Cher," he tells me, hand on my shoulder. He's not mocking; he's protecting. He's going to save me from being a girl. "Don't be Cher," he says, "because *you're not*," in the same tone in which white liberals go to Newark and tell kids they're *somebody*.

"Cher walks like this," he says, "and so do you."

He walks back and forth across the front of the room and swings his hips from side to side and flaps his arms. Part duck, part Mae West. No one laughs. We're stunned by the likeness.

"Now you do it," he says to me.

So I get up in front of the room, in front of everyone, and walk.

I go from one side of the room to the other, from the double doors at the entrance to the grand piano and back, twice.

"Help him out, people," Mr. O says. "What's he doing wrong? Tell him."

My friends tell me to drop my arms and square my hips. Straighten my wrists. After a while, Mr. O stops them and says, "Watch me. This is how a man walks."

The room is tiered and carpeted, and he climbs up one side and across the back and down the other side, showing me how to walk. "Now follow me," he says, and again he circles the room, with me behind him, trying to do what he does. We circle the room until the bell rings.

✳ ✳ ✳

Mr. O and some other teachers form a committee to save me from being a girl. Team of experts. A reclamation project. Speech therapy, weight training, psychotherapy, private counseling.

In the weight room, I work out with the football team. I have to ask them to spot me. I meet with the guidance counselor, who is also the football coach. Ball teams, gym coaches: I'm to be rescued by my attackers.

The speech therapist, Mrs. Reed, sits across from me at her scarred desk and tries to help me make a better S. Apparently, I lisp. She's got a picture book that she spins around to face me. She points at a page.

"What's that?" she says.

"Snake."

"Tongue behind your teeth," she says, wiggling her tongue across her lips and drawing it back to the roof of her mouth. I do the same. We're serpents, darting our tongues. She points at the next picture.

"Sandwich," I say.

"Good," she says, though I can't hear the difference. "What kind of sandwich?" she asks. "Isn't there meat in that sandwich?"

"I'm vegetarian."

She frowns.

"Salami."

"Good," she says. "Now," she says, "put it all together."

"The snake eats the salami sandwich," I say.

"Very good," she says.

* * *

The office of the school psychologist is a log cabin that kids built in woodshop. You have to walk through the boys' gym to get there. My therapist's an undergrad from Fairleigh Dickinson University. His name is Barlow. Love beads and a beard like Allen Ginsberg's. I think I'm his senior project. I spend our sessions shifting between two chairs and having a conversation with myself. In one chair, I'm the Good Boy. In the other, the Dog Boy.

Barlow has a clipboard and a ponytail, and he tugs at his hair and takes notes.

"How do you feel about your mother?"

"I should answer as the Good Boy?"

"You're the Good Boy."

"My mom's okay."

He writes that down.

"What would Dog Boy say? Be the Dog Boy," he says, pointing to the other chair.

My education in becoming a man involves scenes from a Jeff Stryker porno. Tough guys stand over me in the weight room and say, "Push it, queer." College kids want me as their dog.

I move to the other chair.

"I'm the Dog Boy now."

Barlow smiles. "Welcome, Dog Boy," he says. "Tell me about your mother."

I lean forward because I have this idea that a Dog Boy would lean forward.

"Well," I say, "she's okay."

Reaching the guidance counselor means walking through the Mall. Long wide hallway linking the building's two wings, old and new. Cafeteria on one side, library on the other. Along the walls, students hang out in their cliques. From the AV room to the student store, it's: greasers, freaks, AV nerds, farmers, jocks, cheerleaders, and brains. I walk down the Mall several times a day, every day. Everyone does. And each clique has a name for me as I pass. Greasers: "Faggot!" Freaks: "Faggoty fag!" AV nerds—AV nerds! I'm an object of derision even to the

AV nerds—"Gay boy." The farmers: "Girly fag." Jocks keep it simple: "Fag." Cheerleaders: "Don't be so mean to the fag." Brains: "I wonder what makes him a fag."

The football coach/guidance counselor, Mr. Bud, is a compact cheerful white guy with his shirtsleeves rolled above his biceps and a bristly mustache. He bangs me on the shoulder and says, "How's it hanging?" Is he asking me about my testicles? Is that what makes him a man?

* * *

In health class, taught by the wrestling coach, I learn what makes you a *gay* man. "Homosexuals, because of the abnormal sensitivity of their anus," he says, "like to put stuff up there. Up their butt. All the time. It wears out their sphincter before they're twenty-five," he says, "and they gotta wear diapers 'cause they've got the constant runs."

Put something in my *anus*? I'm going to have to wear *diapers*?

* * *

Then at the end of my sophomore year, I'm in a play where I get to be the hurt boy who just wants to say something real.

* * *

The play's *Impromptu*. A one-act. Absurdist and ripped off from Pirandello. Metafictional drama: four actors, two men and two women, are sent onstage by an unseen stage manager and told to stay there until something real happens. Trapped in the light, with a roomful of people staring at them, they argue. What should they do? Are they in a play? What kind of play are they in?

"It's not supposed to be an *imitation* of life. It's supposed to *be* life."

That's one of my lines. I'm Tony, anguished and young. I say stuff like:

"Who are we? Why are we here?"

I turn to the audience and ask *them*: "Who are you? Why are you here?"

"I have nothing to give except myself," I say, "and that doesn't seem to be enough."

I love Tony. Being Tony. I have modeled him on Jane Fonda's performance in *Klute*. She has four improvised scenes with her shrink where she talks about what it's like to be looked at by men. I want to do that, be Jane, tell the truth about myself from a distance. Exposed, but behind the mask of impersonation. Confessional, but protected by dramatic convention.

Our first performance is an afternoon assembly for the freshman class. Seven hundred kids. Maybe a third of them are here. Guys in the front row make fart noises and snap bubblegum, waiting for the play to start.

The house lights dim. Our first few beats are done in the dark. We're "actors," stumbling around, trying to find our way. "Why is it dark; what does the stage manager want?" Then the lights come up, and we can be seen.

And we can see out into the house. Real actors know how to "create their privacy," but I don't. I'm aware of the audience. I'm supposed to be. It's a play with no fourth wall; the audience is part of the action. I spot my mother in the back under the Exit light. She's friends with the drama teacher, and they're standing together, against the doors that lead to the lobby where the school keeps sports trophies in glass cases.

"It's worse than it was before," is my first line after the lights come up.

And a kid in the front row says, "Shut up, faggot."

Everybody hears.

We keep going. Then another kid says, "Gay boy." Out loud.

More kids start talking and laughing. It spreads from the front row to the rows behind it, then throughout the audience, which ends halfway up the auditorium. Then there's empty space, then my mother.

A guy stands up.

"What makes you such a faggot?"

All the boys are laughing, and the girls are laughing too. Kids shout and laugh and chant.

We can't hear ourselves act. We shoot looks at each other but keep going. Maybe the drama teacher will speak. Maybe someone will shut down the lights. The boys in the front row are standing. The kids behind them are yelling. The ones who aren't shouting are laughing.

Then I have to cross downstage and ask them what they want of me.

I'm playing an actor who wants to be real and not an actor. And I'm a kid who wants to be an actor and not real. No; I want to be real as an actor. I think acting is being myself, but safely. Tony's a symbol of my anguish. No one has ever asked me what it's like to be a faggot. To be called a faggot all day long. Not the therapist, not the football coach. Not the health teacher, not the choir director. Not Mr. O. This is my confession, posing as Tony, who doesn't want to pose. I walk to the apron, and look at the audience, and say, "I have nothing to give except myself and that doesn't seem to be enough."

The guy who wrote the play, Tad Mosel, is gay, but I don't know this. He wrote *Impromptu* for his Yale classmates in 1949.

I still don't know anybody gay. Nobody openly gay, no one who identifies as gay. There is no such thing as "identifying as gay." I don't even know anyone who's been *accused* of being gay. You can *only* be accused of being gay and deny it. Nobody *is* gay. I don't even know if I'm gay.

What I know is, I'm telling the freshman class and my mother that I have nothing to give except myself. I'm yelling to be heard. For a second, everyone is quiet. We've crossed the line from art into life, and maybe everyone in the room is savoring the transition. A real moment is taking place in somebody's actual life, in the guise of a performance about people searching for real moments in their actual lives. The levels of irony are way complex. Twenty years from now, I'll be busy, like, "deconstructing" them. Or telling them to a shrink. Right now, though, my main concern is my body: getting out of it. I want to be outside myself. Not high on sex or drugs or God. It's not transcendence I want, but expedience. Like when you're about to be in a car crash, and the smart thing is not to be in your body when it happens.

So I'm out of range, swinging from the arc lights in the space above my head at the moment of impact. Looking down, I can see myself mounted on the stage: arms wide, neck bared, face lit, surrounded like a condemned man on a gallows platform and looming over the crowd. Any moment now, someone will kill the lights. The drama teacher will stop the show. But they let me dangle. I'm hanging in two places, trapped in my body and floating above it, being and leaving myself.

I'm thinking, "There's my gay body." It's my first postmodern moment. My classmates aren't just hectoring me; they're turning me French. I'm a "body" caught in a "contact zone," the "site" where 350 fifteen-year-olds discover their power. I'm the symbol of their fear and their strength.

And look at me: skinny doughy white boy, sixteen years old, dressed for a high school play, wearing greasepaint and powder, eye shadow, eyeliner, lip liner, and rouge, straining and hot under the stage lights, bent forward, trying to connect.

And look at them, red-faced, yelling, "Die, faggot."

I'm thinking, Aren't they tacky? Chicken farmers; they're all their own cousins. That's how I fight back. I'm critiquing them. Maybe that's what "gay" means: "critic." Diapered critic.

I don't want to say I was incapable of mockery or abuse. I thought I was smarter than everyone else, and I let them know it. My father worked in New York!

Kids are cruel; sure.

Tony walks offstage before the play is done. I walk through a door that leads into the hall beside the auditorium, and they stop yelling, and the play goes on, with the actors talking and the audience quiet. And out in the hall behind the stage, it's like it hasn't happened because from that point onward, no one ever says a word about it.

No one mentions it.

No one.

Not a word.

Not ever.

Not to me.

Not the Health teacher. Not the Choir director. Not the speech therapist. Not the Drama teacher. Not the football coach, not even when he was the guidance counselor. Not the student shrink. Not the actors on the stage. Not my mother. Not my friends.

They said nothing and kept calling me a faggot. The weight room jocks said, "Push it, faggot." Mr. O came up behind me in the hall and said, "Watch those hips."

Now we all knew my secret. We knew what I was. We had watched each other knowing. I had nothing to hide or confide. I was the shameful secret you repeat in order to have one. Secrets need to be shared. Everyone said it, named it, discussed it, but me. I was a faggot, a gay faggot. And it was apparently none of my business.

1997–2020: East Village; Montrose; Hell's Kitchen; Flushing; Fishtown; & Gowanus

Biographical Note

John Weir is the author of two novels, *The Irreversible Decline of Eddie Socket*, winner of the 1989 Lambda Literary Award for Gay Men's Debut Fiction, and *What I Did Wrong*. He is an associate professor of English at Queens College CUNY, where he teaches in the MFA program in creative writing and literary translation. In 1991, with members of ACT UP New York, he interrupted Dan Rather's *CBS Evening News* to protest government and media neglect of AIDS. He lives in Brooklyn, New York.

CPSIA information can be obtained
at www.ICGtesting.com
Printed in the USA
JSHW042335210422
25165JS00003B/3